PRAIRIE ROADS

PRIMROSE SERIES
BOOK EIGHT

TANYA RENEE

Serenade Publishing

Serenade Publishing

www.serenadepublishing.com

For Erica, a true survivor and dear friend.

ALSO BY TANYA RENEE

Primrose Series

Prairie Sky

Prairie Nights

Prairie Fire

Prairie Hearts

Prairie Sound

Prairie Rain

Prairie Prestige

Prairie Roads

Prairie Charm

With The Band

Finding Direction

Love Notes

On The Edge Of Forever

PROLOGUE

The road lay before Georgie. The tug of the fresh gravel under the tires of her bicycle made it hard to pedal. She soldiered on, seeing her best friend and neighbour, Brooks Isley, off in the distance, reaching their secret meeting place that no one but them knew about.

Brooks had been her best friend for as long as she could remember. Having grown up across a field from each other, their farms ran parallel, field facing field, and their parents were close friends. From the moment they both learned to ride a bike, they had been holding top-secret meet-ups at the juncture of their two gravel roads. There they would climb down the rocky slope of the ditch and, weather permitting, they would climb inside the wide mouth of the metal culvert, just the two of them, tucked away from any prying eyes. Sometimes they would read books or reenact made-up stories. Other times Brooks would tell her corny jokes, making her laugh until her sides hurt. Mostly, they would talk, sharing their deepest thoughts, hopes for the future and wildest dreams. As they grew up, going from young children to tweens to teens, they navigated the awkwardness of self-discovery together, always reminding each other that as long as they were friends, they could get through anything.

When Brooks got on the bus that afternoon, his eyes downcast and his shoulders slumped, all he had to do was glance Georgie's way and it was understood that they would meet in their place. By the time she reached him, he was laying his bike in the long grass off to the side of the road. Brooks feigned a smile, his face unable to mask his emotions.

"Hey Georgie," he said, his eyes drifting down at the ground as he kicked lightly at the gravel with his favorite Converse sneakers.

"Hey Brooksy," she replied, frowning at his melancholy mood. "What's wrong?"

Brooks flushed, his round face turning red, with a deep blush settling in his cheeks.

"Let's go to our place." Georgie suggested, placing a supportive hand on his shoulder.

He nodded, and they climbed down the rocky embankment, Brooks taking Georgie's hand to keep her from slipping on the rocks. It had rained recently, leaving a mini creek flowing through their culvert, so they opted to take a seat on the metal top, letting their legs dangle over the edge.

Georgie nudged his arm, coaxing him to talk and tell her what was wrong.

Brooks glanced down at his hands, wringing them

anxiously as he did when he was embarrassed and wasn't sure he wanted to talk about it.

"You know I won't tell anyone, Brooks." Georgie assured, meeting his eyes. "You can tell me anything."

Brooks let out a big exhale as he confessed, "I asked Bethany Carmichael to go with me to the junior high dance and she turned me down."

Rumblings of his rejection had gotten back to Georgie, as teen girls loved to talk, and honestly could be mean, but she wasn't about to share that with him as it would only make him feel worse.

"It seems Max Turner likes her too and asked her to the dance before I did, and well, Max is cool and popular, so..."

"So what?" Georgie asked, sitting up straight, and feeling the need to defend her friend. "He's not as funny as you are!"

"Yeah, I know." he sighed, with resignation. "But Max is a jock, and it seems like the girls like the boys who play sports," he said, jutting out his stomach and giving it a slap as he let out another pensive sigh. "Girls don't like guys like me."

"Don't say that, Brooksy," Georgie chided, reaching over, and settling her hand on his forearm. "I happen to think you're cute. Far cuter than most of the boys at school. Plus, you're cuddly and give the best hugs." She added, looping her arm into his, snuggling into his side, and putting her head down on his shoulder as she stared up at him.

Brooks met her gaze, offered her an appreciative smile and rested his head on hers. Their gazes turned to follow the trail of water that flowed below them as they sat together, comforted in each other's company.

Georgie raised her head off his shoulder, her eyes pinned on him and offered him a sincere smile. "Brooks, if someone can't like you for you, then they aren't worth your time," Georgie added, as she slipped her hand into his, lacing their fingers together. She searched his face, trying to meet his gaze.

His eyes drifted back to hers as he conceded, "I guess you're right. I wish all girls were as cool as you are, Georgie," he said, giving her hand a squeeze.

"I know I'm pretty awesome!" she replied, raising her chin up proudly. "Maybe one day you'll have a girlfriend as amazing as me."

"Maybe one day you'll be my girlfriend," he countered, meeting her eyes with amusement.

Georgie slowly blinked at him as the side of his mouth quirked upward in a lopsided grin. They both burst into laughter at the thought, and Georgie shook her head. "I'll tell you what, Brooks." Georgie started, tears of amusement glossing her eyes. "When we're both old, like 30 or something, and if we still don't have a girlfriend or a boyfriend, I'll date you." She said, spitting into her palm and putting her hand out to him.

Brooks looked down at her hand, his eyes lifting to meet hers, a playful hopefulness in their depths as he accepted her handshake and replied, "Okay, Georgie, it's a deal."

CHAPTER 1

Georgette Donahue stared out through the large picture window of her family's farmhouse, taking in the barn, arena and paddocks sprinkled with horses. She loved quiet mornings like this. Early mornings, when the entire house was quiet, when she could sit in the solitude and nurse a steaming cup of herbal tea.

The Donahue farm was always a bustle of activity. With their Equine Therapy business at the core, Georgie, as a licensed psychotherapist, spent her days working one on one with her clients, who were mostly children, and running family therapy sessions on weekends. The children she worked with varied in age and ability. Working with both disabled and able-bodied youth who struggled with behavior issues, depression, anxiety and sometimes, trauma. Seeing her clients build confidence, learn impulse control and emotional awareness was incredible, and when they broke through and a child bonded with a horse, building a bridge of trust, it made all the hours and time spent worth it.

Bringing her mug to her lips, she gingerly took a sip of the hot soothing liquid as her phone buzzed on the kitchen table. Smiling, she set her mug of tea down and reached for her phone, swiping it open. Clicking on the message, it read:

Brooks: Dad Joke of the Day–Which days are the strongest?

Georgie laughed and rolled her eyes at her best friend as she replied.

Georgie: I don't know, Brooks, which days are the strongest?

Brooks: Saturday and Sunday as the rest are weekdays.

Georgie: Groan! Are you running out of material, Brooksy?

Three dots instantly popped up indicating he was responding. Georgie waited with bated breath.

Brooks: My material is endless; you should know that by now! Good morning, Beautiful! Can't wait to party with you this weekend at our 30th birthday celebration. I've been practicing my dance moves, so you better be ready to bust a move!

A GIF of the end dance scene of "Footloose" popped up on her screen, and she giggled. Brooks always knew exactly what to do and say to make her laugh. Biting her lip, she considered her response, a mischievous smile covering her face as she texted.

Georgie: If you can dance like Ren McCormack in Footloose, you'll have all the ladies scrambling to dance with you.

Brooks: Naturally, but you know, Georgie, there's only one lady I want to dance with.

Georgie sighed, reading through his response a second time. He always did this. Left her little comments, insinuating that she was his one and only girl. Brooks was her best friend, and despite keeping him securely in the friend zone, there was no question that somewhere along the way his feelings towards her had turned romantic. Brooks wanted more with her, but was she going to go there with him? Not a chance. She couldn't fathom losing his friendship if they didn't work out, and she wasn't willing to take the risk. Her phone buzzed in her hand.

Brooks: Have a great day, and I'll see you soon!

Georgie read over their conversation again, and sighed, holding her phone to her chest for a moment before shaking her head and setting the phone down on the table. She had to treat his flirtation and comments as a joke, her friend being his usual facetious self. Yet lately his comments landed more serious and with the constant ribbing she received from family members and friends regarding their relationship, it was hard not to take Brooks' comments at face value. It wasn't that she didn't find him attractive. Brooks was incredibly handsome, with his sandy blonde curly hair that he always kept a little longer so his curls would flop over his forehead, making him come across as endearingly boyish. His striking blue eyes were mesmerizing when they changed shades with his moods, and then there was his smile that could light a thousand rooms. Georgie had seen Brooks go from a chubby, insecure kid to a confident big and tall man who, at six foot three inches tall, was strong and hulking from his years working at the local feed mill as an operator. The only thing bigger than Brooks' stature was his personality, charisma and humor, which garnered him countless friends. Simply put, he was everyone's friend and could put a smile on anyone's face. That included hers. She never went a day without a joke or a funny message from him, and considering what she did for a living, he served as the comic relief in her otherwise heavy day.

Hearing the creak of footsteps on the wooden stairs, Georgie glanced to the side as her brother Kolt and his fiancée Jane's sweet laughter filled the kitchen. Jane was six months pregnant and adorably had Kolt's henley shirt stretched over her protruding belly.

"Good morning." Jane said, flipping on the kettle. Kolt reached into the cupboard to pull out two mugs, setting one down in front of Jane, as he leaned in and nuzzled her neck with his morning scruff, making her giggle before making his way to the coffeepot to pour himself a mugful.

Kolt and Jane were never short on PDA, and Georgie loved seeing her brother so happy. Jane had become a good friend, her soon to be sister, and Georgie couldn't have imagined a more perfect fit for him. Although she was immeasurably happy for Kolt and Jane, she would be lying if she didn't feel envious at times seeing them so hopelessly in love. A baby coming in three short months, a wedding planned this summer and plans to break ground on their farm shortly thereafter. They had found happiness in a truly serendipitous meeting, resulting in a whirlwind romance and, despite having gone through insurmountable challenges, they had found their way through it together.

Kolt took a seat beside her, giving her a nudge with his

foot. "Are you excited for Saturday night? I just got an invitation from Brooks to a dance showdown at the GB Corral."

"GB Corral?" Georgie asked with a smirk as Kolt took out his phone and swiped it open.

"Georgie and Brooks Corral, see." Kolt explained, handing his phone to her.

On the screen was a cartoon video, with her face transposed on one cowboy and Brooks face on the other, doing a funny dance to "Cotton Eye Joe". Georgie nearly fell off her chair in a fit of giggles as she shook her head and handed the phone back to Kolt. *Classic Brooks.*

Their mother, Emmaline Donahue, came down the stairs, a wide smile on her face as she took in the laughter around the kitchen table. "Good morning, my darlings!" she sang out, going around the table, dishing out morning hugs and kisses. "What are you all laughing about?"

"Brooks just being Brooks." Kolt said, handing his phone to his mother. She clicked on the video and chuckled before handing it back to Kolt. Shaking her head as she strode over to the coffeemaker, she commented, "That boy has always been funny. Even when he was just little, he would say and do the most hilarious things."

"How long have you all known him?" Jane asked curiously, taking a sip of her tea.

"Oh goodness, we met his parents when Georgie and Brooks were just in preschool. So maybe since they were three years old. His mother, Dorothy, and I started going out for coffee while the kids were in school and became fast friends. It wasn't until a month later that we discovered we were neighbours. We have a lot of wonderful memories with the Isleys." Emmaline replied with a reminiscent look on her face. "Brooks and Georgie were instant friends, and Dorothy and I used to dream that one day they would get married, so we could share grandkids."

Georgie rolled her eyes, having heard this story countless times. She stood up and carried her mug to the sink. Agitated, she turned, pinning her mother with a glare. "For the millionth time, Brooks and I are best friends. That's it and that's all it'll be."

"Friendship is a good foundation for an epic love story, my dear," her mother added, causing Georgie to shake her head and let out an exasperated sigh, knowing that arguing with her was futile.

Striding over to her mother, she planted a kiss on her cheek and met her gaze. "I appreciate your words, Mom, and no matter how much you fantasize, it's

never going to happen, so please lay off it, okay?"

READING over his text to Georgie again, Brooks Isley smiled as he leaned over the granite countertop of his kitchen island. Having moved here a year ago, after his cousin Jaxon Isley completed the last phase of development on the south end of Primrose, his townhome was spacious and modern, and he loved having a space that was all his own. Setting his phone down, he reached for his large travel mug and fixed his coffee the way he liked it, with a healthy splash of cream and a hint of sugar. He took a sip of the coffee, slipped his phone into the front pocket of his Carhartt overalls, and made his way to the front door, reaching for his toque and slipping on and lacing up his steel-toe work boots. Only five more days of work and he had the entire weekend to celebrate with Georgie and their closest friends. Although he had every intention of spending time with everyone who was attending, the one person he wanted to spend the most time with was his best friend, Georgie Donahue. He and Georgie had been friends for as long as he could remember, and for almost as long, he had been head over heels in love with her.

It was a million different things that made him love her. Her beautiful chocolate-brown eyes. Her gorgeous smile with the most adorable dimple. The contagious laugh that he could so easily pull out of her. Her caring heart, her loyalty, her fierce devotion to her work and how she truly listened to him — just a handful on his list. Georgie had his heart, and if only she would open her heart to him, he knew he could give her the life she wanted. Sadly, however, his love for her remained unrequited. She had long relegated him to the friend zone and although he knew that he should let go of the possibility of them being more, something in the depths of his heart, always told him to hold on and not give up on them becoming more.

Reaching for his keys, he heard his phone ding, and he quickly fished it out of his pocket. "Have an amazing day, Brooksy! I adore you."

Smiling, he typed back; *I love you* and he paused his finger hovering over the send button. He had typed those three words countless times when conversing with

Georgie, and so many times it sat there, three sacred words floating between them, just waiting to be said. *Not through text, Brooks. You need to say the words to her face.* Shaking his head, and with a resolute sigh, he backspaced and typed in *I adore you too.*

CHAPTER 2

Georgie entered Everything You Knead, the delicious, enticing smell of fresh-baked cinnamon buns, a feast for the senses. There was a lineup as there usually was on Wednesdays, and she waited patiently as the patrons were served, carrying out their decadent treats in pastel pink boxes tied with string. The couple in front of her having been served, she was greeted by the vivacious owner, Marnie Baxter.

"Hey there, Georgie!" Marnie exclaimed, offering her a bright smile. "Let me guess, you're here for two cinnamon buns?"

"Am I that predictable?"

"Every Wednesday," she replied with a laugh, as she reached for an already prepared bakery box containing the usual order. "You can tell Brooks I put a little extra cream cheese icing on his, just the way he likes it." She said with a wink.

"You know you spoil him, right?" Georgie replied with a laugh.

"He's such a sweetheart, I can't help myself!" Marnie exclaimed as her delighted eyes darted past Georgie to the front door. The door chimed, and in walked a handsome man with fiery red hair and a thick red beard to match.

Georgie watched as Marnie's husband, Davis Baxter, came around the counter and wrapped his arms around her waist, unabashedly pulling her in for an intimate kiss. Georgie couldn't look away. They were so perfect together, their relationship one that she knew had withstood despite incredible hardship.

"You two are far too adorable." George said as she leaned on the counter and let out a swoony sigh.

"Married nine years this month." Marnie replied, wrapping her arms around Davis's waist, and giving him a nostalgic smile.

"Nine of the best years of my life," Davis added, kissing Marnie chastely again.

"I hope someday I can say that," Georgie said, with melancholy in her tone.

"You will. I'm sure the right one is closer than you think." Marnie reassured with a wink as she handed her the bakery box containing the cinnamon buns.

Georgie shook her head and let out a resolute laugh, knowing exactly who she was referring to. *Is this entire town conspiring for Brooks and me to get together?* "Thanks, Marnie." Georgie replied with a roll of her eyes as she turned and exited the bakery.

Making her way down the street, passing Isley Construction and Hastings Hardware, Hayden was outside chatting with a customer. Raising his hand in greeting to her, he shouted, "Looking forward to the party on Saturday. Pickled Pig at 8 p.m.?"

"You got it!" she exclaimed, pointing a finger his way. "I hope you and Whitney are ready to get your dance on!" she added, with a shimmy of her shoulders.

"You know I always am!" he said, busting out a move right there on the sidewalk.

Georgie giggled as she turned the corner to the parking lot of the feed mill, seeing Brooks in the open overhead doorway talking to a fellow employee. As soon as he spotted her, his cheeks rose in the widest smile, and her heart warmed at the sight. Brooks always had a way of making her feel like she was the only girl he could see, and anyone who ended up with him was going to be incredibly lucky. *So why won't you consider him for yourself?*

Georgie was aware that Brooks felt deeper for her than she did for him. He didn't hide it well. And she would never deny that she cared deeply for him too and if she was being honest with herself, she loved him. In the same way he loved her, she honestly wasn't sure. *What if I open that door and it doesn't work out?* Brooks was her best friend in this world, her ride or die, and the possibility of losing him was simply too much to bear.

Walking up the steps of the loading dock, Brooks rushed over to take her hand, his crystal blue eyes twinkling as he greeted her with his usual term of endearment, "Hey there, Beautiful."

Brooks' heart swelled at the sight of her. *My Georgie.* She smiled brightly as he took her hand, helping her up the concrete steps onto the loading dock.

"Hi," she replied, holding out the bakery box, her eyes meeting him with a playful glint. "I got your favorite, with extra icing."

"Oh, that Marnie knows me far too well," he said, taking the box and patting his belly. "I blame Marnie single-handedly for my boyish figure. That and stellar genetics, of course."

Georgie rolled her eyes at him, giggled, leaned in for a hug and patted his stomach. "I hear the dad bod is the pinnacle of sexiness right now. You're going to be fighting off the ladies on Saturday night."

"Only one lady who matters." he replied under his breath, and she gave him a chastising side-eye before he continued. "Perfect timing as always; my break just started."

Gesturing to the loading dock where they usually sat, Brooks set down the box and helped Georgie find her perch before he settled in next to her. A cloud of feed dust lingered in the air around them, and she looked down at his overalls, covered in a light dusting. "Busy day?"

"Always. Really looking forward to having the weekend off, though. Been working a lot of long hours these days and I need to let off a little steam," he replied, as Georgie opened the bakery box and retrieved two forks from her jacket pocket. "Do you want to drive to the Pickled Pig together? I can pick you up."

"I'll meet you at your place if that's okay. The only

problem is that if we drive together, that means one of us can't fully let loose.

"I can take one for the team," he replied, breaking off a big piece of the cinnamon bun and lifting it to his mouth, then rolling his eyes back as he chewed, leaving a trail of icing through his beard.

Georgie shook her head with a laugh, licked her thumb and reached over, wiping the icing from his face. He turned, pretending to try to bite her like a rabid dog, and snarled at her. Georgie's laugh deepened as she gave him an adoring look and dipped her finger into the icing, sucking it off her finger absentmindedly as she gazed out over the parking lot towards Main Street.

Brooks groaned internally , his body immediately responding as it always did around her. Georgie had no idea how incredibly sexy she was, and so many times when they were together, Brooks had to temper his libido. Before he had a chance to get carried away with naughty thoughts, he nudged her arm, bringing her attention to him.

"I was thinking about this birthday the other day, and I thought about a moment we shared in our secret place when we were in 7th grade. I was so heartbroken that Bethany Carmichael turned me down, and to cheer me up, you said if we get to the age of 30, you would be my girlfriend," he said, waggling his eyebrows. "If I do recall, we even did a spit shake on it."

"Funny, I don't remember that part," she said, feigning ignorance.

"Oh, I recall that part vividly," he replied with a deep,

playful laugh. "I'm turning 30 on Tuesday, and you're turning 30 on Sunday. Don't you think it's time to pay up on that deal?"

Georgie slowly blinked at him, her face turning serious. "Why do we need to mess with something that's perfect the way it is, Brooks? You are my best friend, and I couldn't ask for one better. I adore everything about you, but I don't see you as a love interest."

Taking his plastic fork, he mimicked being stabbed in the heart, making a joke of her turn down. Humour was his default for dealing with the rejection. Seemingly oblivious, she giggled and hooked her arm in his as she settled her head on his shoulder the way she always did. "You're the best."

Leaning in, he kissed the top of her head, his heart aching for more with this woman he loved.

* * *

GEORGIE PULLED INTO BROOKS' driveway, sliding out of her SUV and reaching back onto the passenger seat to retrieve a gift bag stuffed full of colorful tissue. She smoothed her hand down her red satin camisole and straightened her jean jacket as she strode towards the door. Pressing the doorbell, she laughed as the unmistakable sound of Chewbacca echoed through the door. The front door swung open, and Brooks smiled his impish smile as Georgie peeled with laughter on his front stoop.

"That's some doorbell, Brooksy," she said, dabbing the tears of laughter from her eyes.

"A little gift to myself. Do you like it?" he asked, stepping back for her to come into his entryway.

"I love it. Suits you perfectly," she added as she held out the gift bag to him. "I know it's not your birthday quite yet, but I just made a little something for you."

He took the gift and wrapped her in a big bear hug, her entire body melting into his. Brooks always gave the best hugs, like a large teddy bear, so soft and cuddly. She inhaled the spicy scent of his cologne and instantly felt a wave of comfort and familiarity wash over her. Releasing her from his embrace, he scanned her up and down, taking her hand and making her twirl for him as he let out a little whistle of admiration.

"Georgie, you look sexy!" he complimented. "Like a red-hot country vixen."

"You think?" She asked, her smile growing wider and the dimple in her cheek deepening. "I didn't want to look like I was trying too hard."

"You look perfect, beautiful," he replied.

"Thank you." She said, going on her tiptoes to plant a kiss on his cheek. "You clean up nicely too." She said, taking in his untucked light blue button-up shirt that brought out his eyes, over a white t-shirt and dark wash jeans topped off with his brown cowboy boots. She glanced back down to the gift bag in his hands. "Are you going to open your gift?"

"Heck, yeah, I am!" he exclaimed, setting it on his kitchen island and making a show of removing the tissue paper and tossing it over his shoulder one by one.

Georgie buzzed with anticipation. "I hope you like it. It's just something cheesy I made for you."

He pulled out a photo album and glanced up at her, his blue eyes wide as he turned back to his gift and took in the picture of the two of them as kids on their bicycles. "You made this?" he asked as he started to page through the book, each a favorite photo of the two of them chronicling their almost three-decade long friendship. She nodded, her heart feeling full as his smile grew wider with each page he turned and with each comment and chuckle at the photos she selected. He got to the end of the album, the last page blank, and he looked up, meeting her eyes.

"I left the last page blank so we can add a picture of us tonight." She said, staring up at him earnestly.

His face morphed from joy to something Georgie couldn't identify. He looked away quickly, his Adam's apple bobbing as he swallowed down hard, and when he returned his gaze back to hers, shiny with tears, she wasn't sure what to think, so she asked hesitantly, "Do you like it?"

Brooks cleared his throat gruffly and met her expectant gaze, full of so much adoration her breath caught. "Georgie, this is the most amazing gift anyone has ever given me," he managed, emotion edging his voice. "Thank you; I'm speechless."

"Brooks Isley, speechless," she replied, her voice dripping with sarcasm. "Somebody mark this day on the calendar."

Brooks let out a laugh, his booming chuckle echoing through the kitchen as he pulled her in for another hug, kissed her on the head and replied, "Smart ass."

* * *

PULLING into the parking lot of the iconic Pickled Pig Honky Tonk Bar in St. Augustine, they were greeted by the classic neon winking pig wearing a cowboy hat. Their eclectic party of family and friends had arrived and were waiting outside the bar for them. The Hastings brothers with their wives, his Isley cousins Jaxon, Drew, Cade, Walker, and Owen along with their significant others, Kolt and Jane and his sister Falyn, who had just moved back to Primrose from the West Coast.

"The party has arrived!" Brooks shouted, throwing his hands up in the air as he let out a loud whoop.

Georgie shook her head and laughed as they were met with birthday wishes and hugs. Georgie quickly found Falyn, the only other single in their group, as everyone entered the building, the loud bass of "Need a Favor" by Jelly Roll blasting over the speakers as the bar filled up fast. The owner, Sylvio, waved from behind the bar and pointed to a corner booth that had a large reserved sign on it. Their party made their way across the dance floor to the booth where several seated themselves, others opting to stand. Georgie surveyed the room, feeling large hands graze her waist, and she turned, her cheek brushing Brooks' facial scruff and making an unexpected aware-ness spark through her body as he asked, "Would you like a drink?"

Smiling up at him, with his blue eyes vibrant even in the dim light of the bar, she nodded. There was never a need to ask her what she wanted. He knew her preference was a good old-fashioned beer.

Georgie's eyes followed Brooks as he crossed the dance floor towards the bar, finding herself admiring how handsome he looked tonight. But when her traitorous eyes roamed down his body, appreciating how fantastic his butt looked in his jeans, she frowned and internally scolded herself. *Georgie, what the heck? You never look at your friends like that.* Shaking her head, she cleared her throat, trying to dispel her inappropriate thoughts.

It had been three years since she had been in a relationship and two years since she'd had sex. A quickie in the backseat of her SUV after a night of drinking after a university alumni night with a man she knew all of three hours. She wasn't proud of that night. A night outside her norm, finding herself caught up in the compliments and attention. She would never forget the look on Brooks' face when she shared with him what she'd done. They had always told each other everything, talking about every relationship and tryst, but something in the way the light in his eyes dimmed with her confession made her realize that their relationship had changed. That was when she became aware of Brooks feelings for her. Perhaps this sudden shift in the way she was seeing him was due to her lack of recent amorous activity. *Yes, that must be it.*

Distracting herself from that disconcerting thought, Georgie surveyed the crowd, checking out the other possibilities tonight. A handsome man in a black cowboy hat caught her eye at the booth next to them, his intense gaze meeting hers. She responded with a flirtatious smile as he ran his gaze over her body appreciatively and flashed her a sexy grin, causing a rush of warm heat to rise from her core. Glancing down, Georgie tucked her hair behind her ear shyly. A little 'hard to get' play, having always worked well for her. Just as she looked up, a blonde in a flirty, skintight mini dress slipped her arms around his neck and planted a not-so-subtle kiss on his lips in a brazen display of PDA. Georgie frowned with disgust and internally groaned as Brooks' sister; Falyn came up beside her, glancing in the direction of the couple now in a full-blown make-out session.

"Fuckers," Falyn said, squinting her eyes at the randy couple. "We don't need to see that."

Georgie let out a guffaw of laughter, never having heard Falyn swear like that before, and put her arm around her, asking, "Good to be back?"

"So far, so good. I wish it were under different circumstances, but yeah, it's nice to be home." She replied.

"I'm glad you're back. And the bed-and-breakfast is opening soon?"

"Five weeks." She replied. "The place needed some upgrades and some aesthetic improvements, but otherwise it was ready to go. The kitchen is amazing, though! A literal dream to cook in!"

"I can't wait to taste all the delicious food from that kitchen. Everything you make is incredible, Falyn," Georgie complimented.

Falyn Isley was a certified chef who moved back to Primrose after a messy divorce from her cheating restaurateur husband. Although the circumstances of her return were tumultuous, she was able to acquire the bed-and-breakfast on the edge of town, fulfilling a lifelong dream.

Brooks returned, three drinks in his large hands, two beers and a Coca-Cola for Falyn.

"I should be buying for the birthday boy," Falyn said, taking the drink from him with gratitude.

"Just happy to have my big sister back home," he replied, looking down at his sister with adoration.

Petite Falyn, stretching to a whopping five foot five inches, wrapped her arm around her much taller brother and beamed up at him.

Brooks and Falyn had always been close, just like Georgie and Kolt were. Although in their case, the Isleys were closer in age than she and Kolt were, with Falyn only 18 months older than Brooks. Sometimes Georgie wondered why she hadn't ended up being best friends with Falyn rather than Brooks. Her conclusion was that Brooks and she were always meant to be.

Taking a pull of her beer, she held it close to her chest as she nudged Brooks with her hip. "Any prospects here tonight?" She asked, wiggling her eyebrows at him.

His eyes drifted over the room but quickly returned to her, meeting her gaze with a languishing twinkle as he replied, "Just one."

* * *

KNOWING he was making Georgie uncomfortable; he cushioned his comment with a joke. Holding out the beer bottle in his hand, he jested, "She's smooth, curvy..." He slid his finger through the condensation accumulated on the bottle. "... a little cold and she has some bite, but I love her anyway."

Georgie giggled and swatted him on the arm as he smirked, and took a long pull on his beer, letting the cold bitter liquid numb his longing for her.

It had always been like this. Him pining after her and

Georgie taking his remarks and innuendos as a joke. They were supposed to be together; he was sure of it. Even though she didn't see it, safely keeping him in the friend zone, Brooks was never going to give up on making Georgie his girl. She had been claimed, and he was simply biding his time until she recognized it for herself.

"Let me take a picture of you two!" Falyn exclaimed as she retrieved her phone from her purse.

Georgie immediately curled herself around him, her arms slipping around his waist. Brooks was used to Georgie's affection, with it simply being part of her personality, but having her this close sent shockwaves through him. A palpable surge of agonizing attraction that made him want to lift her into his arms and plant a scorching kiss on her lips.

"Kiss her!" Hayden shouted from their booth, which elicited a chant from their guests of "Kiss her, kiss her."

His eyes darted to meet Georgie's, whose brown eyes twinkled with amusement. With a raised brow, Brooks gave her a questioning look. Georgie smiled, and before he knew it, Georgie jumped into his arms, her hands hooked around his neck. Brooks' eyes widened, his heart pounded out of his chest as Georgie looked him in the eye, their hot breaths mingling.

"Let's appease the peanut gallery, shall we?" she said as she inched closer, and his eyes closed in anticipation of her kiss. *This is it. This is the moment.* The softest lips planted a kiss, lingering next to his mouth, and his stomach fell as disappointment washed over him. *Rejection.*

Boos and jeers sounded from their group as Georgie

unhooked herself from Brooks and wrapped him up in a hug. He wrapped his arms around her despite wanting to slink away in embarrassment. Georgie pulled away, glancing up at him, the look on her face speculative as she surveyed him. But he couldn't hide his defeat in that moment, and Georgie's face instantly fell.

CHAPTER 3

The bar grew louder; the music filling the air along with the raucous laughter from their group. Brooks was in full force, entertaining everyone with his antics and jokes, and Georgie's sides hurt from laughing. It was always this way with Brooks, his charismatic personality filling up the room. Brooks had been putting on a show, masking the disappointment she had seen in his eyes earlier that night. Georgie wasn't so cold-hearted that she hadn't seen how her rejection affected him. Part of her wanted to kiss him, give in to the pressure from their friends and simply plant a kiss on his lips. But the logical part of her brain took over, and she couldn't do it. She couldn't cross that line knowing how much it would mean to Brooks. *But would it mean something to me? Would kissing Brooks change the way I feel about him?* The thought of that scared Georgie. She loved what they had, and changing their dynamic had the potential to ruin their friendship.

Brooks eyes landed on hers, and she smiled at him

apprehensively as she lifted her beer to her lips and took a long pull. He slowly sauntered over to her, adding a little extra swagger to each step, making a smile tug at her lips. Reaching her, their eyes locked, and he put out his palm and flashed her that award-winning smile. She accepted it and ever so gracefully stumbled to her feet as the dizzying buzz of alcohol went straight to her head.

Brooks caught her, his hands strong around her waist as he steadied her on her feet. "Dance with me, light-weight." Brooks said as he swung her around and brought her back to him, slipping his arm around her and guiding her to the floor.

They found an open spot on the dance floor, Brooks pulling out his best moves, making her giggle as he went into 'the sprinkler' chasing it with 'the shopping cart'. The music slowed as a Brett Young ballad filled the room and dancers coupled up. Several of their friends and family with their respective others joined them on the floor until it was a sea of couples swaying to the swoony love song. Brooks turned his gaze to Georgie and made a grand bow to her as he asked, "May I have this dance?"

She curtsied awkwardly, almost losing her balance, and answered, "It would be my pleasure, kind sir."

Brooks laughed, taking her hand, and pulling her into him, his large hulking body eclipsing hers as they found their rhythm. Stealing a glance at him, she couldn't help but admire the man who held her in his arms. Brooks really was a good-looking guy with his amazing blue eyes, rugged stubbled chin and the curly dark blonde hair that kept flopping endearingly into his eyes. His gaze met hers as a flash of amusement glinted there.

"What are you looking at, Beautiful?" he asked, pulling her hand in close and sandwiching their laced fingers between them.

"I'm just looking at how handsome you are," she said, staring up at him dreamily as her smile turned to a look of conviction. "If the girls can't see it, well then, fuck them!"

Brooks let out a deep, rich laugh as he returned his gaze to hers, pure folly on his face. "I think you may have your beer goggles on, Georgie."

"That may be," she admitted with a slight slur in her words. "But I think you're a catch and can't understand why you're still single."

Brooks continued to sway with Georgie in his arms, the feel of her body flush with his, heady and making his thoughts jumble. Despite the sting of rejection earlier, he was going to relish this moment between them and make it last as long as she allowed.

"I mean it, Brooksy!" she continued in exclamation. "You are so cute, so smart and soooo funny! You have a great job and your own house! You Brooks Isley, you are a fucking catch!"

With another chuckle he replied, his eyes trained on hers, "Maybe I'm waiting for someone special."

"Yeah. I get that," she said sadly, her intoxicated roller-coaster mood drifting to melancholy as tears started to well up in her eyes and she choked out. "It's hard to find someone special."

Brooks let go of her hand and tipped her chin, raising

it to face him, her eyes now glossy with both the libations and this sudden onslaught of sadness. "You listen to me, Georgette Donahue. You are the definition of special. Anyone, and I truly mean anyone, would be lucky to be with you. Never doubt how truly awesome you are," he said with conviction in his tone. "You, Georgie, are one in a million."

Georgie blinked at him a moment, a slow smile sweeping across her face as she slurred out, "I love you, Brooksy."

Now it was his turn to slow blink, but even though she had never uttered those words to him before, he knew if she was in her right mind and not in a drunken stupor, she would have regretted it. Despite this, he wasn't going to miss his opportunity to reciprocate.

"I love you too, Georgie. More than you know."

* * *

THE NIGHT WOUND DOWN, most of their group helping them shut down the bar. Brooks held Georgie securely around the waist, knowing she was long past the point of too much.

"Are you good to drive, mister?" She asked, her words coming out adorably slurred as she poked him in the chest with her finger.

"I only had one beer at the beginning of the night." He replied, opening the door for her, and picking her up to set her down on the seat. "I promised you I would get you home safely."

"You did, that's right!" she exclaimed, her hands

coming up to cup his face as he leaned over her and buckled her seatbelt. Surprised, Brooks met her eyes, so rich and dark, shining brightly in the light of the parking lot. Suddenly, she leaned in and planted a kiss on the edge of his lips, her hot breath feathering his skin as she pulled back. "Oops, I almost kissed you again," she whispered, bringing her hand to her mouth, and stifling a giggle.

"I wouldn't have minded." He replied with a waggle of his eyebrows. "Although the first time I kiss you, I'd prefer you not to be inebriated."

His comment not completely landing with her drunken state, Georgie threw her head back against the leather seat and scrunched up her nose. "I know I smell like a brewery..." she struggled to say, eliciting a laugh from deep in his chest.

With her safely buckled, he rounded the truck and climbed in, his eyes roaming over to the gorgeous woman in the passenger seat, with her sleepy eyes locked on him.

"Did you have fun tonight, beautiful?" Brooks asked, reaching over, and brushing her hair off her face.

"I did," she replied, a sleepy smile curling her lips as her eyes fluttered closed. "I had the best time.'

BROOKS PULLED into his driveway and put his truck in park. The steady rhythm of Georgie's light snoring was the only sound filling the darkness of the truck cab. Brooks unbuckled and shifted in his seat to face her, laying his head against the headrest. Taking in her serene face and long lashes that fanned out on her cheeks, he reached out and smoothed his fingers down the side of her face, reveling in the softness of her skin as her eyes cracked open and she sucked in a stilted breath. "Are we at your place?" she asked groggily.

"We are." he replied. "Did you want me to take you home, or are you spending the night?"

"Can I spend the night?" She asked, meeting his gaze with sleepy eyes.

"Of course, Beautiful," he replied. "Let me help you inside."

Brooks climbed out of the cab and came around, opening the passenger-side door, scooping her into his arms. She felt light as a feather as she nestled against his chest. Reaching into his pocket, he pulled out his keys and fumbled to open the door. With the door finally open, he locked it behind him and climbed the stairs to his second-floor bedroom. Although his townhome was a two-bedroom unit, he used the extra space for storage, so tonight he would give her his bed. It wasn't the first time she'd spent the night, and he was more than happy to take the couch and give her his space and privacy. Setting her gently on the bed, he crouched down and met her half-mast eyes.

"Do you want to wear one of my shirts to sleep in?" he asked as he helped her remove her cowboy boots and set them next to the bed.

She nodded, and he strode over to his dresser, opening a drawer. Rummaging through it, he smiled when he found his favorite Johnny Cash Man in Black T-shirt. A gift Georgie had given him years prior.

"Will this work for you?" he asked as he turned around and his breath caught, his eyes growing wide.

There was Georgie, her red camisole having been discarded to the floor, with just a satin and lace push-up bra making her curves swell out the top. She was in the process of kicking off her jeans, and all he could do was watch as she revealed a very skimpy pair of matching underwear before she collapsed back onto the mattress. Brooks groaned internally, willing himself not to look, but his betraying eyes had a mind of their own as they roamed boldly over her half-naked body, and all blood ran south, his jeans instantly feeling uncomfortably tight.

Get yourself together, Isley. Taking a deep breath, he walked back over to her, trying to overt his eyes as his brain went wild, telling him to just look his fill. *You've seen her in a bikini before. This is no different.* With that thought in mind, he brought his gaze back to her.

"Georgie, you need to sit up so you can get this on," he said, putting his hand out to her.

She took his offered hand, he helped her to a sitting position, and she looked up at him, her brown eyes so beautiful it made his head spin. Giving him a look of gratitude, she curled her arms around her back and before he realized what she was doing her bra was slipping down her arms, exposing her creamy breasts and tight dusky nipples. His cock stood at attention.

"Fuck me," he groaned under his breath as he handed her the shirt and quickly looked away. Giving her a moment, he hesitantly turned back to find her sitting on the edge of the bed, now fully covered by his shirt. Her head hung low; he crouched down in front of her.

"I drank too much tonight." She said, meeting his gaze.

"I know, Beautiful. Are you going to be sick?" he asked, his brows furrowing with concern.

"No, I just need to sleep," she replied, turning to crawl onto his bed, his shirt riding up over her hips and giving him a far too fantastic view of her scantily clad backside.

With a sigh, he pulled back the covers for her, and she climbed in, sliding her legs under the comforter. Covering her, he leaned down and kissed her head, her lips curving up into a smile. Rising to his full height, he strode over to the dresser again and pulled out a T-shirt and basketball shorts, then walked to the door, glancing back at her. She raised her head off the pillow and asked, "Where are you going?"

"I'm going to sleep on the couch," he replied.

"Don't be silly, there's plenty of room." She said, scooting her body over to the other side of the bed.

Unable to help himself, he asked playfully, "Is this your way of seducing me?"

Georgie giggled, her voice raspy from a night of shouting over the loud music of the bar. "Stop Brooksy. You and I have had sleepovers before."

"Yeah, when we were ten and camping in the back-yard." He exclaimed, closing the bedroom door, flicking off the lights, then turning on the bedside lamp.

"Think of this like camping," she replied, her heavy, sleepy eyes closing again.

He set to work unbuttoning his shirt and sliding it down his shoulders, leaving him shirtless.

Georgie whistled, her sleepy eyes watching, her voice rough and groggy. "Hot stuff."

Heat settled in his cheeks, the way it often did when around Georgie. He unbuttoned his pants, sliding them down his hips, leaving him in his boxers, his body still fully appreciative of Georgie's brazen display of nakedness. Glancing over at Georgie with the hope that she hadn't noticed his rather obvious arousal, he found her with her eyes closed, drifting off to sleep. He slipped on his t-shirt and shorts and entered the ensuite, preparing for bed. Reaching for his toothbrush, he took in his reflection, his voice of reason going wild inside his head.

What are you doing? Georgie is your friend; your best friend, and she wants you to sleep in the same bed as her. As much as you want her, she doesn't feel the same. Her flirtation tonight is just the beer talking. You can't read more into it than that.

Attempting to shake off the swirl of thoughts running through his head, he took his time finishing up his bedtime routine, and when he opened the ensuite door, Georgie was fast asleep. Pulling the covers back, Georgie had turned on her side facing away from him, allowing just enough room for him to slide in next to her. As soon as he covered himself and reached over, clicking off the lamp, he turned and Georgie had scooted back, her small body bridging any gap between them and curving into the groove of his large one. He closed his eyes, a low groan reverberating through his chest as he tried to figure out where to place his hand. *To hell with it,* he told himself as he settled his large hand on her stomach, and she sighed, snuggling into him more. With the heat of her body feeling like it was meant to curl into his, he sighed in reply, closing his eyes and letting the sweet scent of her honey shampoo lull him to sleep.

* * *

WAKING up wrapped around the large trunk of Brooks' body was a new experience for Georgie. Part of her wanted to protest and deny the fact that she'd asked him to sleep with her last night. But she'd remembered it, the drunken words coming out of her mouth and the look on his face when she asked him too. She crossed a line last night, each little part coming back like a slow-motion film reel. Almost kissing him in his truck, Brooks carrying her into the house and up to his room. Brooks retrieving his t-shirt and her stripping…. *oh God. Pretty sure I flashed him my boobs and gave him a pretty good view of everything else.* Georgie groaned internally, remembering the expletive that had escaped his mouth. *Georgie, you are such a tease.* She didn't want him to get the wrong idea. As the memories of last night came back to her, so did her shame and embarrassment. She considered simply sliding out of his bed and slipping out before he woke. But he was too warm and cuddly, so she snuggled deeper into him, her nose feeling fuzzy from the blissful contentment of being held in his arms. Glancing up at him, his face was turned towards her, his curly hair covering one eye and his deep breaths exhaling in a low rumbly snore. She rested her hand on his chest, swirls of dark blonde hair peeking through the V-neck of his T-shirt, as her head rose and fell with each breath in and out. She buried her head deeper, relishing the closeness she hadn't felt in… *have I ever felt this?* Her eyes drifted back to his to be met with one impossibly blue eye open and watching her.

"Stop that!" Georgie exclaimed, peeling herself from his body and covering her head with the comforter. "It's so creepy."

Brooks laughed deeply at her reaction to his party trick, his whole body shaking the bed as he joined her under the covers and turned to face her. "Happy Birthday, Georgie."

"Thanks." she replied. "I can't believe I'm 30."

"You're older than me!" he said, cocking an eyebrow at her.

"By two days!" she added, swatting his arm playfully, then smoothing her hand over the reddened skin. Brooks chuckled and met her eyes. "I guess I thought I would have had my life locked and loaded by now. A husband, maybe a kid, I don't know. Just further ahead than I am," she said, her voice taking on a wistful tone.

"I feel the same way. I seriously think I would rock the husband and father gig."

Georgie grinned in agreement. "You'd be the best dad."

"Heck, yeah, I would," he replied, taking her hand in his. "But there's still time for all of that."

"I know." She said, lacing her fingers with his as a somber silence fell between them. They lay like that for a moment, in quiet reverence, until Brooks, in true Brooks fashion, broke the heavy silence. "What do you give a 3,000-pound rhino for its birthday?"

"I don't know." She replied with a giggle.

"I don't know either, but you better hope he likes it!" he exclaimed, causing them both to shake with laughter.

Georgie wrapped herself back around Brooks in a hug, and he reciprocated by wrapping his arms around her.

"Brooks, you always know how to lighten the mood."

* * *

As was tradition, Brooks pulled a red velvet cake out of the refrigerator and set it in the middle of the large kitchen island on a cake platter. Georgie loved old movies, "Sixteen Candles" being one of her favorites, so every year since they were 16, they recreated that iconic scene from the movie with Molly Ringwald and Michael Schoeffling, minus the kiss of course. Now, with his own place, they didn't need to suffer the incessant teasing from family as they did it. Brooks chuckled at all the times they sat across from each other on kitchen tables, large cake between them, forks poised to dig in, and snickers in the background as family watched in the wings. But despite the remarks and laughter at their expense, they never missed a year; this tradition was one he cherished.

Hearing footsteps at the top of the stairs, Brooks retrieved two forks from the drawer and set them beside the cake as he pulled out a BBQ lighter and quickly lit the candles just as Georgie rounded the staircase and entered the kitchen. The lights were out, blinds drawn, only the glow of the candles lighting the space. Georgie's face brightened as she bounced on her toes and clapped her hands excitedly.

Brooks loved making her smile like that as he admired how gorgeous she looked with her shoulder-length hair damp and curling around her naturally beautiful, makeup

-free face. She was still in his huge T-shirt and had slipped her jeans back on from last night. Everything about Georgie radiated warmth and beauty, and as he took her in, he was as always in awe.

"You are so beautiful," he said, almost breathy, and her eyes met his as they flashed with amusement and darted down to his oversized shirt covering her body.

"I hope you're not too attached to this shirt." She said. "Because I think it's mine now."

"Consider it part of your birthday present then." He replied. "Now come over here so I can give you your actual birthday gift."

Georgie rounded the island as Brooks reached for a small gift bag tucked into the corner. His heart was beating a mile a minute as he nervously handed the gift bag to her, and she beamed up at him. Watching her slowly open it, his pulse quickened, and his mind reeled with a million questions. *Is it too much? Is she going to think I'm overstepping our friendship? Will she even like it?* Pulling out a small wooden box that he purchased from Hayden, with a rose carved on the front, she opened it slowly to reveal a delicate gold bracelet. Her eyes darted up to his, a swell of emotion rising within them as she lifted the bracelet and read the small plaque, "Beautiful. Oh, Brooksy, this is..."

"Read the other side," he urged. She turned the bracelet over in her hands, and engraved into the gold was "Love, Brooks." She blinked, staring at the gift, her fingertips smoothing over the engraved words.

Shit. Now I've done it. She's going to take this as me pres-

suring her into more. But I do want more. I want so much more. I want her. I want a life with her.

With the silence growing thick, he felt a sense of panic rise in his chest, and he had to fill it. He had to fill the silence fast. "There wasn't enough room for them to put "Love your best friend, Brooks," so I..."

"I love it." She blurted out, interrupting his explanation. "I'm just speechless, that's all. No one has ever given me something so wonderful."

Brooks let out a long breath he hadn't realized he'd been holding and reached out to help her put on the bracelet, his hands taking on a nervous shake as he fastened the clasp. Georgie noticed, took his hands in hers to steady them and smiled up at him, her cheek sinking into the deepest dimple. "I adore you, Brooks Isley," she declared as she went on her tiptoes and planted a chaste kiss on his cheek. "Thank you."

Feeling a warm flush where her lips had touched his cheek, he released her, clapped his hands together and rubbed them eagerly. "Okay. Beautiful, hop up here onto the island. We got a birthday cake to eat!"

* * *

ENTERING THE BARN, Georgie was greeted by Jane, who was busy feeding the horses. Her barn jacket was unbuttoned, no longer able to cover her burgeoning baby bump, and she was wearing one of Kolt's Donahue Farms t-shirts underneath along with a pair of his old sweatpants. Jane's cheeks and tip of her nose were rosy and pink from the cool early spring morning.

"Good morning." Jane greeted as she took a seat on a bale of hay and took in a deep breath as she rubbed her bump.

"Good morning." Georgie replied, taking a seat next to her. "Where's Kolt?"

"He had to run into town this morning." She replied. "He wanted to talk to Jaxon about the plans for the farm build. I opted to stay back."

"Ahh... he's finally going to get started on that." Georgie said, nodding her head.

"Right after the wedding." Jane beamed as she changed the subject. "Hey, thanks for a fun night on Saturday. I can't remember a time when I've laughed that much. Your friend Brooks is awesome." Georgie smiled, her fingers playing with a gold bracelet on her wrist. Jane's eyes followed the movement and drifted back up to meet her gaze, a smirk curling her lips. "That bracelet is so pretty. Is it a birthday gift from Brooks?"

"It is. He surprised me with it on the morning of my birthday. It was so sweet. He was so nervous giving it to me, and he's never like that," she said as she flipped the plaque over and touched the engraved words there. Jane leaned over to read the inscription.

"He really loves you." Jane said. "It isn't hard to see from the way he looks at you."

"We're just friends." Georgie answered quickly. "I'm not going to lie and say I haven't thought about it. I mean, he's truly the sweetest, funniest, greatest guy in the world, but if we cross that line, it has the potential to ruin a life-long friendship. I don't think I could risk that. I couldn't imagine losing him or not having him be part of my life."

"I get that; I truly do." Jane commented, "But what if it does work out and you two end up together? Wouldn't that be worth the risk?"

"I don't know." Georgie answered truthfully. And she didn't know. It was hard to think of Brooks in that context. She had always looked at him through the eyes of a friend, never letting herself see him as boyfriend material. It was hard to imagine kissing, touching, making.... Her face started to flush, but her body seemed to heat at the thought. *You can't go there.*

CHAPTER 4

As the grass started to turn green, the April rain subsided and settled into the warmth of the impending summer. Georgie sat on Brooks' back deck, enjoying a glass of iced tea as she read her romance novel and glanced up, watching Brooks exit his shed with a push mower. She loved afternoons like this. Nothing to do, nowhere to be, just her, a good book and her best friend. They had spent countless afternoons like this over the years, just the two of them doing everything and nothing. Georgie lifted her book, reading a particularly spicy part of the novel as she heard the mower fire up. As the protagonist swept the heroine into his strong arms and carried her up the grand staircase to his bedchambers, Georgie flashed back to how Brooks had carried her up the stairs to his bedroom, the night of their birthday celebration. *It really is so incredibly hot when a man can just pick you up like you weigh nothing. So hot when their strong arms bulge and strain as they carry you, so firm and taut under your fingertips. Damn, you need to get laid, Georgie.* She bit her bottom lip as she read on, her imagination turning the main characters into her and Brooks as he laid her out on the bed, towering over her and he unbuttoned his shirt, slowly, sexily undressing. Imagining Brooks expansive chest, broad strong shoulders, hulking arms and the light dusting of manly hair that sprinkled down his chest and stomach leading to a delicious trail from his belly button, disappearing into his jeans. He reached for his belt buckle, unfastened it, and pulled the belt out in one smooth, dominant motion. Her face flushed at the thought of Brooks unbuttoning his jeans and sliding them over his hips, the black briefs underneath barely containing the impressive erection within. Her breath hitched as he curled his fingers into the sides of his underwear, sliding them down inch by painful inch, revealing his massive....

"What kind of smut are you reading?" Brooks asked, swiping the book from her hands.

"Brooks!" she squeaked in protest as he turned the book around and read aloud the part she was reading.

"*Reginald laid Miriam out on the bed, the velvet of her ripped bodice framing the milky skin of her exposed breasts and torso, framing her figure like a piece of fine art to be admired.*" Brooks looked up from the book, pure folly dancing in his blue eyes. "Why, Georgette Donahue, you hussy," he teased with a waggle of his eyebrows as Georgie rose from the patio table and lunged for the book. Pulling it away before she could grab it, he continued. "*You are exquisite, and I want to devour every inch of you, my love.*" Brooks let out a whistle. "With those fancy words, he might seduce me too."

"Brooks, stop!" Georgie giggled, conceding, and taking her seat, her face beet red with embarrassment.

"*Reginald towered over her like a lion — proud and fierce, his hands pulling at the ascot around his neck...* oh fancy indeed." Brooks said, mimicking a British accent as he settled into a seat across from her and continued. "*He undressed slowly, his eyes locked on the precious jewel splayed out before him, and when he stood before her bare, his long thick manhood revealed, she swallowed down hard, her eyes widening at the gargantuan size of him.*"

"It does not say that!" Georgie giggled.

"Basically, it says Reggie is packing, so I'm taking some creative liberties here as an interested reader." Brooks replied with a mischievous smirk. "Let's see what he does with that massive dick of his, shall we..." Brooks read on, now to himself, suddenly bringing his hand to his chest and letting out a gasp. "If I had pearls, I'd be clutching them. Reggie is showing Miriam how they do it in jolly old England. Wow, well done, Reg!"

"Brooks, you're incorrigible." Georgie said, shaking her head, her face a burning inferno as she leaned back against her chair.

"I try." he winked, his blue eyes sparkling playfully as he finally handed her back the book. "Is this the kind of literature 30-year-old spinsters read nowadays?"

She gave him a chiding look, only making him smile wider. "No, but when you're single, don't have a prospect on the horizon and you haven't had sex in two years that isn't battery operated, you have to get your rocks off somehow."

Brooks slowly leaned forward, resting his elbows on

the patio table as he met her gaze with a coy smirk. "You know I would be happy to help you end the drought."

"Brooks, fuck off!" she exclaimed, reaching over, and slapping his shoulder with her book.

"Just thought I'd offer my services." He said as he leaned back, stretching his hands up in the air as he settled back against the seat and folded his hands behind his head, letting out a contented sigh. "Man, I love days like these. Weather is just starting to turn, the smell of freshly mown grass in the air, hanging out on the patio with my favorite girl. Life doesn't get much better."

Georgie smiled, deeply inhaling the clean spring air as her phone buzzed, startling them both and Georgie picked it up, reading the caller ID.

"It's a text from Kolt," she said, looking up at Brooks and then back down at her phone. "He said, Jane's water broke, and they're on their way to St. Augustine General Hospital. Mom is with them."

"Isn't that too soon?" Brooks asked, his face morphing to concern.

"Two weeks early, but that's not bad. Baby must be ready." She said, sending Kolt a quick text back and setting her phone down on the patio table with an excited smile.

"You're going to be an aunt." Brooks said brightly as he leaned over the table and put his hand out to her.

Georgie accepted his offered hand, his entire palm making her hand disappear. *When did his hands get so big?* Something about it was oddly comforting. He gave her hand a squeeze, breaking her from her obscure thought, and she grinned at him.

"Why don't I pull out some steaks and we can BBQ tonight?" he said, meeting her gaze. "We can enjoy the rest of this beautiful day on the patio and stay on baby watch."

"Sounds perfect to me."

* * *

FROM THE MOMENT Georgie held her nephew, Gatton Patrick Donahue, in her arms, she was in love. Born at five pounds, three ounces, he was simply tiny perfection, and she couldn't get enough. They were all sitting around the kitchen table, Kolt cradling his little curled-up body in his arms, when she saw Brooks' truck pull into the drive. Rushing to the door, Georgie opened it just as Brooks was climbing the stairs onto the porch, and he laughed deeply as she took his hand and dragged him inside.

"Hold up now." Brooks chuckled at her eagerness. "Let me take off my shoes."

Brooks had a large stuffed teddy bear under his arm, and he handed it to her as he slipped off his shoes and hung up his jacket and then turned to her. "Okay, Uncle Brooks is here. Point me in the direction of the little nugget."

"Just in the kitchen." She said excitedly as he handed him back the teddy bear and they made their way towards the open space of the kitchen.

Georgie's mother greeted him with a big hug, and he said his hellos to Kolt and Jane, his eyes zoning in on the bundle resting against Kolt's chest. He leaned down, peering at his little scrunched up face, and rose to his full height, declaring, "I haven't been around too many babies, but I have to say, he's pretty darn cute. I brought him a teddy bear as I didn't know what you bring babies to be honest, but when I saw this portly fella, I thought it kind of looked like me so..." Brooks held the bear up and grinned wide, producing a laugh from everyone. "... this bear is either going to scare the kid or remind him of his uncle Brooks or both, I don't know," he said with a smile as he handed the bear to Jane.

"Thank you, Brooks. Did you want to hold him?" Jane asked.

"Ah, yeah, sure." Brooks replied, nervousness tainting his tone as he took a seat at the head of the table next to Kolt. Carefully, Kolt handed Brooks the infant, and Georgie watched as he carefully positioned him in his arms. Gatton instantly started to fuss, and Brooks' eyes widened, looking around for direction.

"Just support his head and hold him against your chest. He seems to like that position the best." Georgie's mother stated as she helped Brooks get him into position. Georgie sat back in her chair watching Brooks hold the tiny infant against him, her heart growing as his eyes lifted and met hers, a big smile curving his lips as he looked down at Gatton, adoringly saying. "Hey there, little man."

"Isn't he perfect?" Georgie cooed.

Brooks leaned down and kissed his little head, his gaze drifting around the room, then back to the tiny baby in his hold. Georgie watched him intently, loving how small Gatton looked against Brooks' large chest, trying hard not to swoon. With a look of wonder in his eyes, he carefully eased back in the chair, Gatton's adorable little squished face looking happy and content. Georgie's heart felt full, and the familiar pangs of want enveloped her. The desire to have a child of her own took over.

"You're a natural." Emmaline Donahue said as she set a coffee cup in front of him and glanced at Georgie, the look she gave her saying, "Are you seeing what I'm seeing?" Georgie rolled her eyes and brought her attention back to Brooks holding her nephew, and when their eyes met, she could see emotion in their depths. The empath in her reached out and touched his arm. His gaze settled on her hand a moment before he cleared his throat and looked up at everyone watching them.

"What do you call a baby potato?" Brooks asked, his eyes dancing with mirth. Everyone's smiles widened as they waited for the punchline. "Small fry," he answered softly as he planted another sweet kiss on Gatton's tiny head.

* * *

HOLDING SUCH a tiny baby today was messing with Brooks' head. He had been tossing and turning since he turned out the lights, his mind going a mile a minute. He couldn't get the look Georgie gave him out of his mind as she watched him hold Gatton. The look held the usual adoration she had for him, but there was a deep longing there and something he had never seen from her before: true, honest love. He was certain that's what he saw. The look had made him emotional, his feelings almost spilling over.

Turning he flicked his bedside lamp on and rolled out

of bed, making his way to the ensuite. Gripping the countertop, he looked up, staring at his reflection. *I'm not bad-looking. A little rough around the edges, but otherwise handsome. Why isn't Georgie attracted to me?* For years he had chalked it up to them growing up together and seeing each other through every awkward coming of age phase, bad fashion choice and terrible haircut. But now, at 30, he liked what he saw in the mirror. Yeah, he could probably stand to lose 50 lbs, but honestly that didn't bother him. He was big, strong, and tall. *Aren't there women out there who find that attractive?* It wasn't like he didn't notice women turning their heads and looking twice when he walked into a room so obviously; he did have something going for him. Turning on the faucet, he leaned down, splashed cold water on his face and reached for a towel. *Had he had his blinders on for too long with Georgie being the only one he saw?* Brooks loved her and likely always would, but he wanted someone to reciprocate his love, desire him, and want to be with him always. Build a life and a family. Georgie had made it abundantly clear that she wasn't going to be that for him, and as he stood there meeting the eyes of his reflection, a wave of resignation washed over him. *You need to move on from her. It won't change anything. You will always stay friends.*

Brooks exited the ensuite and took a seat on the edge of the bed, reaching for his cell phone. Swiping it open he flipped through it, his eyes zoning in on the app that had been there since he was 18. Clicking it open, he created a profile, answered all the questions, and uploaded a photo ironically that Georgie had taken of him. Finished, he set his phone down, climbed back into bed and flicked off the lamp. *It's time to take control of my future.*

* * *

GEORGIE HADN'T SEEN Brooks for two weeks. He had cancelled their weekly cinnamon bun dates, telling her he had too much work and that he had to raincheck. Although it wasn't uncommon for him to be busy like this, something kept niggling at the back of her mind that he was avoiding her. After the day he came by to meet Gatton, he had been distant and quick to respond with short, clipped answers, and now she was starting to miss him.

Closing the box stall after her last therapy session, she pulled her phone out of her back pocket and swiped it open, typing out a quick text to Brooks.

Georgie: Got plans, Brooksy? I was thinking pizza and a movie. What do you think?

Brooks: Sorry I can't.

Georgie: Why not? My treat!

Brooks: I have a date. Raincheck?

A date! Georgie frowned, her stomach dropping. *Brooks is dating. When did this happen?* Georgie swallowed hard. Brooks told her everything, and his dating again was big news. *Why didn't he tell me?* A wave of unexpected emotion enveloped her, and her throat constricted painfully, making it hard to breathe. She leaned against the wall, looking down at her messages again, trying to breathe in and out slowly to calm herself. *Why am I having such a visceral reaction to this news? It's not like I have a say in what he does and whom he sees. It's not like I have staked a claim on him.* Yet despite all the facts, in that moment, deep down in the pit of her stomach, it felt like she was losing him.

With Kolt and Jane's wedding only a week away, Georgie had been busy with preparations for the past month, lending a hand to whatever task she could to keep her hands and mind busy. She had seen Brooks only a handful of times, their exchanges very surface level, her big, jovial, flirty friend not coming out to play. It wasn't until Kolt told her that he was seeing someone from Winnipeg that she understood why. Brooks was shifting his time and energy onto someone else, and if he was happy, she was happy for him. *But am I?* The truth was she missed him terribly, and not having him around as much made her think about everything that was lacking in her own life. She didn't date and only had a handful of truly close friends, most of whom were married off or paired up. Without Brooks around, she was truly alone for the first time in her life.

Deciding to drown her melancholy in one of Marnie's decadent cupcakes, Georgie pulled up to the bakery and exited her SUV. When she entered the place was quiet, so she decided to sit inside rather than get a cupcake to go. A perky teen greeted her and took her order before handing over the red velvet cupcake piled high with cream cheese frosting and a herbal tea. She took a seat at a table looking out onto the main street. Lost in her own thoughts and relishing the comfort of her favorite treat, Georgie stared out at the street, watching the cars drive by and familiar faces pass as they walked along the side-walk. There was only one familiar face she wanted to see. *Brooks.* A swell of emotion caught in her throat, and she quickly lifted her hot tea to her mouth and took a soothing sip. *You're being silly*, she scolded herself. *It's not like Brooks has fallen off the face of the earth.* With a deep sigh, the bakery door chimed, and Georgie looked up to see Falyn step inside. Falyn walked over to the counter, leaning in to talk to the girl at the front counter, before she turned, her gaze meeting Georgie's. With a bright, acknowledging smile, she strode over to Georgie's table. Falyn gestured to the empty seat across from her and, with a nod from Georgie, she took a seat. Before she could greet Georgie, Marnie's head peeked out of the swinging bakery door.

"Just give me ten minutes, Falyn," she said. "I almost have your order ready."

"Sounds good." Falyn responded before bringing her gaze back to Georgie, surveying her forlorn face then glancing down at her half-eaten cupcake. Her brows drew together as she gave her an empathetic look, asking carefully. "How are you doing?"

Crappy. Sad. Lonely. Her mind populated countless words to describe how she was feeling in this moment, but not wanting to lay her cards out to Brooks' Sister she answered simply, "I'm fine."

"You don't look fine." Falyn countered, leaning her elbows on the table. "What's going on, Georgie?"

Damn her for being so perceptive. Georgie's eyes drifted from Falyn to stare out the large storefront window, and her chest tightened painfully as she confessed. "I'm feeling like a complete loser."

"Georgie." Falyn chided, reaching across the table to place her hand on hers. "Don't say that. You're one of the most amazing people I know."

Georgie let out a little guffaw. "Being amazing doesn't exactly translate to dates," she replied as her gaze returned to the world outside the window.

They sat for a moment, an atypical silence falling between them until Falyn asked. "Does this have anything to do with Brooks dating Kaitlyn?"

Georgie's eyes flitted back to Falyn. "Kaitlyn?" she asked. "Is that the woman he's seeing?"

"Yeah, I only met her last week. She's nice enough, pretty, very quiet though. Not really the type of girl I could imagine Brooks with over the long term, and I'm not sure he's happy with her."

"What makes you say that?"

"Do you want the honest answer or the answer you want to hear?" Falyn volleyed.

"Honest," Georgie answered, swallowing down hard, her head swirling from this information.

"She's not you." Falyn answered, her eyes pinning Georgie, as Marnie came through the swinging door of the kitchen, interrupting their conversation. Falyn rose from the table and walked to the counter, paid for her order, then with bakery boxes in hand turned back to Georgie.

"You should know that Brooks didn't invite Kaitlyn to Kolt and Jane's Wedding. He didn't even consider it." Falyn informed. "Don't you think that says something?"

With that truth bomb, she turned and exited the bakery, leaving Georgie's mind reeling and her conflicted heart waring with emotion.

* * *

IT WAS REHEARSAL DINNER NIGHT, everyone meeting at Prairie Charm Bed and Breakfast to celebrate Kolt and Jane. Georgie had been looking forward to this event for days, not only to see the finished bed-and-breakfast or to enjoy Falyn's amazing cooking but to finally spend an evening with Brooks.

Georgie pulled a cornflower blue dress from her closet and held it up, remembering how much Brooks loved this color, and tossed it onto her bed. With the motion, a sharp stab of pain radiated through her armpit, and she groaned, lifting her arm up and running her finger over the tender skin. The skin felt bumpy, a rash developed seemingly overnight, and she analyzed it for a moment in the mirror, feeling annoyed that it might show when she wore her bridesmaid dress for the wedding. Pressing the tender skin, she felt something hard under her fingertips. A lump the size of a marble but more torpedo-shaped. She pressed on it; the lump gave way like a fat deposit. She had experienced lumps before, usually during her monthly cycle, all going away within a few days. *It's nothing. Probably just a hormone change. You have been on a rollercoaster of emotions lately.* She reached for her housecoat and wrapped it around her as she strode into the bathroom to retrieve some allergy medication, popping two from the pill pack and swallowing them down easily. *Hopefully, this rash goes away before the wedding.*

BROOKS WAS ANXIOUS, attempting to look cool and collected as he shoved his hands into the pockets of his dress pants. He hadn't seen Georgie in weeks, and although they texted daily; he had kept his distance over the past two months. They seldom saw each other, and when they did, it was uncharacteristically brief, chaste, and stiff. Not the usual shared chemistry and banter.

Falyn had scolded him as only a big sister could for the way he was treating Georgie, telling him about seeing her at the bakery alone, wallowing in a red velvet cupcake. His heart hurt painfully when she told him, and a deep chasm of guilt bore into his chest. The last thing he wanted Georgie to feel was abandoned. She was still his best friend after all and, if he was being honest with himself, still someone he desired. *Shit. I shouldn't be thinking this way about Georgie. I'm dating someone. Kaitlyn is so sweet, and kind, and she really likes you. But do I like her as much as she likes me?* Brooks knew the answer, and guilt filled his chest as a resounding 'no' echoed through his thoughts. It wasn't fair to string Kaitlyn along, and now, as he stood here taking a deep, pained breath, nervous to reunite with his best friend and the only woman he ever loved, he couldn't help but think, *you need to let Kaitlyn go.*

From the corner of his eye, he saw the front door open and Georgie walk in, his breath catching as he took in the flowy calf-length blue halter dress that dipped low, exposing the expanse of the creamy skin of her back. She was breathtaking, and he wanted nothing more than to stalk over to her, pick her up into his arms and spin her around, making her laugh. *God, I've missed that giggle.* Mustering restraint, he slowly strode over, her eyes darting around the room and then catching on his. A slow smile curved her lips, making the dimple he loved so much indent her cheek. *Man, I've missed that smile.*

"Long time no see. How are you doing, beautiful?" he asked, his eyes locked on hers.

"I'm good. Excited for the wedding tomorrow." She said casually, letting her eyes roam over him, taking in his semi-formal attire of a light blue button-down shirt and black chinos with a coy gleam in her eye. "You clean up nicely."

"Thanks. You wow, Georgie, you look stunning." he countered, unabashedly looking his fill at his stunning friend, and meeting her gaze.

"What? This old thing?" she said, swishing the skirt back and forth with a cocked eyebrow, her face morphing to seriousness as she confessed, "I've missed my best friend."

"I know I'm sorry. I've..." he began, only to be interrupted by her placing her hand on his chest and pinning him with her chocolate brown eyes. The simple heat of her touch made his heart hammer wildly.

"It's okay, Brooks. I'm happy for you." She said, patting his chest. "I hear you're dating someone named Kaitlyn."

I feel like a douchebag. "Ah yeah, well, it's not serious or anything. No labels, just dates. That's all."

"You've introduced her to Falyn, and your family, so you must be a little serious." Georgie pointed out, calling his bluff.

"I guess."

"Are you dating anyone else?" Georgie asked knowingly, putting her hand on her hip and pinning him with her stare.

"No, just her," he replied, already feeling sheepish.

"Then you're exclusive and probably coming across more serious than you think. Trust me. Kaitlyn probably thinks you're her boyfriend." Georgie said with a resolute shrug. "And because you didn't invite her to the wedding, what do you want to bet she's sitting at home confused and upset right now?"

Brooks stared at her dumbfounded. Georgie always had a way of making him see things from a different angle. Swallowing down the lump of guilt in his throat, he asked, "Do you really think so?"

Georgie didn't answer him, but simply shrugged and walked away.

Brooks ran his hand through his hair the way he always did when Georgie schooled him. *Am I giving Kaitlyn mixed signals? Kaitlyn is a sweet woman. Kind, thoughtful, family and goal oriented, she wants the same things I want, which is to settle down, get married and start a family.* But the reality was there was little to no spark, their conversation lulled, and every time he told her a cheesy joke, she would just feign a smile. Not even laugh. *Crap. I'm an idiot. A dirty dog who's been stringing along a perfectly wonderful woman, only to deny my feelings for my best friend.*

Brooks glanced around the room, everyone taking their seats at a long family-style table set up spanning the length of the dining room. Falyn caught his eye, and she gave him a look asking, 'Are you okay?' He let out a long exhale, nodded in response and found his seat next to Georgie, his head reeling with the reality check that had been thrown into his face.

For the next two hours, they enjoyed the most incredible meal, and despite their earlier conversation, he and Georgie fell back into their usual chemistry and banter with ease. They laughed with the wedding guests as he commanded the room with his charm, wit, and humour. It wasn't until Georgie reached for his hand under the table, feathering her fingers with his, that the warm, soothing, familiar feeling she always brought him returned after far too long. He held her hand in his, so small in his large palm, and all the feelings he'd been casting aside for the past couple of months, in his attempt to move on from her, came flooding back. *There is only one woman I want, and it's Georgie.*

After dinner, the guests lingered, spreading throughout the guest house as he and Georgie stepped out onto the back patio where it was quiet.

"That was an incredible meal." Georgie commented on a long exhale as she sat on the loveseat.

"My sister sure can cook," he replied as he settled in next to her, putting his arm casually around her shoulders.

"I missed you." Georgie said, looking up at him, her beautiful brown eyes meeting his. "Life isn't the same without you in it, Brooks.'

"I'm sorry again that I've been so MIA," he apologized, pulling her into him and planting a kiss on her head. "I guess I was feeling a little weird about this whole dating thing, and I wasn't sure how to talk to you about it. I don't know."

Georgie sat up, turning to face him, her eyes radiating sincerity as she spoke, "Please never feel like you can't talk to me. You are my best friend, Brooks. You can literally tell me anything. If you're happy and have someone special in your life, I want to be a part of that. I want to see you happy."

This woman. How can I feel for anyone else the way I feel for her? Emotion edged the surface as he swallowed down, trying to tamper down the love threatening to boil over. Georgie brushed the curls from his forehead and smiled up at him, his traitorous eyes immediately zoning in on her lush lips, as the desire to kiss her overtook him. But before he could lean in and give in to the impulse, she turned her face and rested her head on his shoulder, curling into him, her sweet honey scent, the consolation prize.

IT WAS Kolt and Jane's wedding day, and the Donahue farm was a bustle of activity. Between her duties as part of the wedding party and rushing around the yard to make sure all the last-minute details were complete; Georgie was put in charge of getting the horses ready for the ceremony so by the time she got the horses to the meadow she was exhausted.

"Are you feeling okay?" her mother asked as she leaned against the kitchen counter nursing a large glass of cold ice water. "Have you eaten at all? You look pale, sweetheart."

"I had a quick lunch, and I'm fine. It's just been a long day so far." Georgie said. "Plus, my underarm is driving me crazy. It's extremely tender, and I have this red, swollen rash there that doesn't seem to want to go away."

"Let me take a look," her mother said, as they stepped into the laundry room for some privacy. Georgie pulled off her shirt and lifted her arm, showing her mother the rash.

"That looks a little angry. You know, I think if we put a little aloe on it, it should help heal it up. Let me go snip some off the plant." Her mother suggested, a firm believer in that old remedy.

Her mother slipped out of the room, and Georgie touched the spot, wincing. The rash hadn't spread, luckily, but it was uncomfortable. *If it doesn't go away by next weekend. I'll go to quick care and get it checked out,* she told herself as her mother slipped back in with a cross-section piece of aloe vera plant. Dabbing the jelly on the rash, it soothed the sting a little, and her mother met her gaze, her eyes questioning. "How are you doing otherwise?"

"How do you mean?" Georgie asked.

"I mean, with all these changes around here," her mother explained, meeting her gaze. "Kolt and Jane having a baby, getting married..."

Her mother had a way of reading her thoughts, and right now she didn't want to give in to the emotion rising in her chest. "I'm fine." Georgie answered quickly, her voice on the verge of cracking. "I'm so excited for Kolt and Jane is wonderful. It's going to be a beautiful day."

"Agreed," her mother said, her eyes searching hers with motherly love. "I just worry about you sometimes. I know how much you want to have what they have, and I know how impatient you can be sometimes. I just don't want you to compare yourself to them. Love will find you when the time is right. There is a plan for you, Georgie. Have faith in that."

Georgie felt emotion painfully constrict her throat as she took in her mother's loving words. Her mother was right; she needed to be patient, bide her time as there was someone out there for her. For the first time in a long time, Georgie felt hopeful.

APPROACHING THE BAR, Brooks scanned the tent, a plethora of familiar faces dancing, laughing, drinking and visiting. The community of Primrose had come out to celebrate the joyous day. Brooks' eyes scanned the tent looking for Georgie. Seeing her walk down the aisle as part of the wedding was enough to bring back every single pang of longing he had carried for her over the years. She was unbelievably beautiful in her yellow sundress, her hair pinned back in pretty curls. It made his breath catch and his heart flutter at the sight of her. After last night, he realized he was kidding himself if he thought he could just snuff out his feelings. Georgie was everything he wanted in his life and more, so when he got home, he called Kaitlyn and explained that he had unresolved feelings for someone else, and they broke up. She took it well, telling him that she figured that they were done when he didn't ask her to join him at the wedding. Georgie was right. She was always right. The only thing she wasn't right about, was that he wasn't the guy for her and last night when he said goodnight to Georgie, her body fitting so perfectly against his when they hugged, he vowed he would do whatever it took to pursue her affections.

Spotting her by the dessert table, he crossed the tent, sneaking up behind her. "Hey there, Beautiful."

She turned around slowly, a napkin with a red velvet cupcake in her hand, and a radiant smile on her lips. Before she said anything, she dipped her finger into the thick cream cheese frosting and brought it to her mouth, sucking off the digit, her eyes never leaving his.

Sweet Jesus.

"Hi" she said, beaming up at him. "I was wondering where you went."

"I was wondering where you went too. I should have known you'd be by the cupcakes." He laughed knowingly.

Georgie shrugged, lifted the cupcake to her mouth, and took a big unapologetic bite. Brooks shook his head as she chewed and licked the icing off her lips. Brooks eyes followed the sweep of her tongue, wishing so much that he could lean in and kiss her. Taste the lingering sweetness of the icing on her sweet mouth. "We haven't been to our secret place in a long time; we need to meet there one day." Georgie commented, looking out over the dance floor.

"All you have to do is call," he replied, watching her take another bite and letting out a little chuckle. "You have some icing, right over here..." he said, taking his thumb to gently wipe away a bit of icing stuck to the corner of her top lip. With the action, Georgie's eyes met his, and he swore he saw a flash of desire there. *Kiss her, kiss her,* his internal voice chanted. Drawing closer, their eyes locked. Static from a microphone sounded, breaking the moment and causing Georgie to take a tentative step back. Their eyes followed the sound to see Hayden behind the DJ booth with a microphone in his hand.

"I know we have a bunch of country music fans here, but let's switch things up for a bit and take things back all the way to 1991. Brooks Isley, this ones for you," he said, pointing in Brooks' direction.

"I'm Too Sexy" by Right Said Fred blasted from the speakers and Brooks waggled his eyebrows at Georgie, his shoulders starting to shimmy as if uncontrollable as he backed up towards the dance floor. "Pardon me, Beautiful, my fans are waiting for me," he said as he turned, strutting onto the dance floor, the guests parting to make a runway for him.

* * *

GEORGIE'S MIND was a confusing hodgepodge of thoughts at the realization that she and Brooks had shared a moment. A moment when she was sure he was going to kiss her. The way he looked into her eyes, and leaned in, the heat of his body so close to hers, made her incredibly aware of how large and masculine he was. *This is your friend, not a love interest. Get yourself together, Georgie.* Pushing back her jumbling thoughts, she focused on Brooks as he strutted his stuff and shook his tush on the makeshift catwalk. She had seen him dance to this song countless times over the years, but his quirky brand of comedy never got old. She let out a giggle as everyone around her whooped, hollered, and cheered him on. *God, I love him.* The thought passed so seamlessly through her mind, but before she could unpack the thought, the song switched to a classic Meatloaf song, and Brooks pinned her with his crystal blue gaze, crooking his finger, beckoning her to the dance floor. With a bright smile, she obliged, joining her best friend as they danced and sang out the lyrics at the top of their lungs, everyone on the dance floor joining in. After several retro classics, Hayden slowed things down as the raspy voice of Joe Cockers, "You Are So Beautiful" filled the tent and Brooks questioning gaze met hers.

"Will you dance with me, Beautiful?" he asked, his eyes sparkling at her in the dimming light of day.

Transfixed, she took his offered hand as he twirled her around, eliciting a squeal of delight from her throat. Pulling her flush with his body, with his large palm resting on the small of her back, the heat of him so close utterly intoxicated her. They swayed to the music, Georgie melting into the feeling of being in his arms as she rested her cheek against his chest. Everything about Brooks made her happy and safe, and she relished the contented feeling every time he was near. *He's not yours,* a niggling voice reminded her as she pulled her head back to look him in the eye and said. "You know after last night's conversation, I kind of expected you to show up with Kaitlyn today."

His eyes narrowed a bit, his mouth straightening into a resolute line as he replied, "Kaitlyn and I decided to go our separate ways."

"Oh, I'm sorry. Are you okay?" Georgie asked, with genuine surprise and concern for her friend.

"Yeah, totally. It was mutual. I don't think she and I had that spark; you know?"

"Chemistry is important."

"Agreed," he replied, pinning her with his gaze as he went on. "I think the right one is going to not only be sweet and compassionate but has a feistiness and can hold her own. I think she's someone who is empathetic to others and cares deeply for her family and friends. She needs to be funny and understand my cheesy sense of humor." His smile grew wider as he finished. "And she must be a complete, hopeless romantic. I'm talking romantic movies, romantic music, romantic novels..." he trailed off.

He's talking about you. Georgie couldn't look away, his eyes so penetrating and so full of conviction. Her mouth dried, causing her to swallow hard as she managed to reply, "Brooks, I..."

His large hand left her waist and came up, cupping her cheek tenderly, silencing her protest, and she couldn't breathe, the feel of his palm too wonderful against her soft skin. "I'm not hearing any more excuses, Georgie. I'm officially throwing my hat into the ring. I want to be with you and be more to you than just your friend. I know you're scared of ruining our friendship and maybe you don't see how well we could be as a couple now, but I want to show you. I want to be given a chance, and I'm not giving up. I'm in this for the long haul, Georgie, and I'll be right here waiting for as long as it takes for you to finally see how good we can be."

Georgie blinked, meeting his earnest gaze, and she couldn't think of the right words to respond to his declaration. She cared so deeply for Brooks, but could she ever see him as her boyfriend or perhaps in the future as her husband? That was what Brooks was talking about. He wanted the future, and he wanted it with her. Suddenly Georgie felt overwhelmed, an onslaught of questions and doubts tangling her thoughts. "I... I need to go," she stuttered, pushing away from him, her eyes not meeting his as she turned and walked off the dance floor.

"Georgie." Brooks' voice sounded behind her as she briskly walked out of the tent, and he reached out, catching her hand, causing her to spin around to face him. With that sudden motion, she felt dizzy, her head starting to spin, but his hands were there on her waist steadying her. "Beautiful, are you okay? You look like you're gonna pass out."

She blinked slowly, trying to get back her equilibrium, and looked up at Brooks. "Sorry, I've just been so tired lately." She replied with her double vision clearing, but her body suddenly felt heavy and exhausted. "It's just been a long day. I think I'm going to call it a night. Can you tell my mom that I've gone to bed?"

"I can, but should I help you inside?" Brooks asked with deep concern etched on his face.

"No, no, I'm fine." She reassured him, patting his chest and offering him a faint smile. "You go have some fun. I think I just need some sleep. Good night, Brooks."

Turning, she strode towards the farmhouse, Brooks parting words cutting through the night, "Good night, Beautiful."

CHAPTER 6

aiting rooms are the worst. Georgie thought as she waited to be called into her doctor's office. After the wedding weekend, she woke up still exhausted, the rash still swollen, and the pain in her underarm irritatingly worse, so she called and immediately made the earliest appointment she could with her personal physician.

"Georgette", a young blonde nurse called as she stood following the nurse into an exam room. "The doctor will see you shortly." She said, placing her chart in a holder on the door and closing it behind her.

Georgie looked around the room, taking in the personal photos on the desk and certificates on the wall. She had been seeing Dr. Edmundson for years and always enjoyed seeing the pictures of her family as they grew. The door opened, and a tall, slim woman in her late 40s walked in, wearing a white lab coat over classic blue scrubs. Her dark blunt cut bobbed hair swung in perfect motion as she took a seat at the desk, clicked her mouse around a few times and then turned to face her. "So, what brings you in here, Georgie? I don't think you're due for your physical until next year." She said curiously.

"I have this strange rash under my arm that's super uncomfortable. At first, I thought perhaps it was an allergic reaction to something, just an irritation, but no matter what I do, it hasn't gotten any better."

"Okay, let's take a look. Can you hop up here on the exam table and take off your shirt for me?"

Georgie did as she asked and lifted her arm. The doctor slipped on plastic gloves, squinted and carefully touched the sensitive swollen spot, which made Georgie wince.

"Sorry, I can see how this would be bothersome. Do you do regular breast exams?" She asked, meeting her gaze.

"I try to, yes."

"I would like to do an exam. Are you okay with that?"

"Yes, that's fine." Georgie replied. "Did you need me to lay back on the table?"

"Yes, please remove your bra and lay back on the table, and I'll do an examination just as I do during your physical."

Georgie removed her bra and lay back on the table as her doctor felt around the affected area. As she pressed into the affected tissue, pain radiated through her armpit and side, making her grit her teeth.

"I'm almost done." She promised as she finished up her examination. When she was done, she helped her sit up, and Georgie reached for her clothes, redressing as the doctor took a seat at the computer, immediately typing.

When she was fully dressed, the doctor gestured for her to take a seat next to the desk. "Georgie, I'd like you to go straight from here to the lab to get some bloodwork done. We're going to check your estrogen levels. I'm concerned as there is a lump in the middle of the affected area, and I think it's in your best interest to have a mammogram done as soon as possible."

"That doesn't sound good." Georgie replied, her eyebrows furrowing as she swallowed down hard, a combination of anxious concern and confusion rising in her chest.

"Have you had any other out of the norm symptoms?" the doctor asked, clicking around on her screen.

"I've been exhausted lately and a little lightheaded."

She nodded. "Yes, let's get you in for the bloodwork today, and I can get you in for the mammogram on Wednesday. I'll email you the details of your appointment." She turned, meeting her eyes with compassion. "I'm glad you came in, Georgie; things like this should always be taken seriously."

IT HAD BEEN five days since the wedding, and Brooks hadn't heard from Georgie. The silence had been deafening between them, and even though he had texted her daily; she hadn't responded, which wasn't like her. *Have I messed things up between us?* He kept replaying the events of that night over and over in his head. How she walked off the dance floor and how overwhelmed and exhausted she looked when he caught up with her. As the days passed and the anxiety built, he felt guilty. So incredibly guilty that he put that on her the way he did. Brooks knew Georgie well, and overthinking was her default. He should have eased into sharing his feelings, but when he locked onto her beautiful brown eyes, he was overwhelmingly compelled to say it. Confess it all to her. Now days later, even though he regretted the outcome, he couldn't bring himself to regret finally telling her how he felt about her. The deep longing desire to be more with her had been closeted far too long. He'd given her plenty of time to sit with his words, and now he needed to know where she stood on them and what she was thinking.

Pulling into the Donahue Farm, he parked his Truck by the barn, thinking Georgie was probably inside either grooming the horses or working out her plan in the office for the following day's therapy sessions. Entering the barn, Brooks looked around and spotted Emmaline Donahue in the feed room.

"Hey there, Mrs. Donahue," he said as he made his way inside the barn. "Is Georgie in the office?"

"I haven't seen her for a while, and last time I saw her, she had climbed onto her bike and was heading down the driveway." Emmaline replied with deep concern etched on her face. "She could really use a friend, Brooks. This has been a heavy week."

"How so?" he asked, his brows furrowing in confusion.

Emmaline met his gaze, her eyes taking on a shine, like she might cry, and instantly his heart sank as she replied roughly. "Just go find her, and she'll explain everything."

Brooks nodded and turned, jogging out of the barn towards his truck, knowing exactly where Georgie had gone. His chest felt tight with worry as he reached the gravel road and turned. Halfway down the mile road he spotted her bike, partially covered by the long grass on the edge of the road. As he suspected, Georgie had gone to their secret place. Pulling off to the side of the road, he parked and exited his vehicle, a sense of urgency to see her consuming him.

"Georgie, Beautiful, are you down there?" he asked, looking over the edge of the ditch. A tinny echo of a whimper answered followed by the sound of crying and his heart fell to the pit of his stomach as he hurriedly climbed down the rocky embankment to the metal culvert below, the sound of her sobs getting louder as they reverberated in the cavernous tube. Crouching down, their eyes met, hers red and puffy, her face streaked with tears.

"Georgie," he said softly as he tried to maneuver his large body into the wide mouth of the metal tube. She scooted back, giving him more room as he bent his legs and wedged himself inside. Her sad eyes meet his, and when they did, it was as if a faucet had been turned on; her eyes instantly filled up with tears.

"Beautiful. What's wrong? Please don't cry," he choked out as he reached for her, wrapping his arm around her shoulders. She snuggled into him, burying her face in his chest, her shoulders shuddering from her sobs. "Please tell me what I can do."

Georgie looked up at him, pure anguish in her eyes as she answered. "They found a lump."

"A lump?" he questioned, his throat tightening painfully. "Where?"

"In my breast, under my arm. I'm going for a biopsy on Monday," she replied, burying her face into his side. "They think it could be cancerous."

"But it could be nothing," he countered quickly, his head trying to catch up with what she was telling him.

"With the other symptoms, my blood work, and now the mammogram, it doesn't look good, Brooks," she replied, her voice breaking as her palm came up wiping at her tear-streaked face.

Brooks tried to swallow, his throat now dry, his head spinning as he opened his mouth to say something, anything, but no words came out. Questions started popping into his head, so many questions with no answers. The only question he could manage came out in a burst. "Do you want me to go with you?"

Her eyes darted up to meet his. "Are you able to do that?"

"I'm sure if I talked to my manager today, I could get the time off."

"Then yes, I want you there," she replied, clinging to him for comfort. Pulling her tight to him, she cried against his shoulder as he kissed her head affectionately, praying to God this was all just a bad dream.

GEORGIE SAT in the exam room chair, her entire world shattering with one ominous word: cancer. A numbness enveloped her, her body outside itself, as each syllable came out of her doctor's mouth in slow motion.

"Before you can start treatment, we need to get you in

for a full-body CT scan, full-body bone scan and MUGA scan for your heart." Georgie nodded; not really hearing the words being told to her. "The results of those scans will go to an oncologist, who will provide you with a treatment plan, which will include chemotherapy, and depending on the stage of cancer you're in, possibly radiation. Your oncologist will explain everything and let you know the next steps."

Georgie nodded again, her body frozen with shock, everything that was just told to her seeming like a mish mosh of foreign words and phrases she didn't fully grasp.

"I'll email you with the next steps and the dates for the tests as well as your appointment with the oncologist. Basically, the sooner we get a plan in place and get you into treatment, the better." Her doctor continued.

Georgie stared at her, feeling her eyelids slowly open and close, open and close, each tiny movement so deliberate.

"I know you must feel a sense of anxiety and shock over this, Georgie. You did the right thing coming in early. Early detection is key in cases like this. It will take a day or two for all of this to absorb, and if you need to talk to someone, there are support groups and therapists I can recommend to help you get through this." she said handing her a brochure and leaning forward, and meeting Georgie's blank stare. "I know this a lot, Georgie, please reach out if you have any questions."

Georgie let out a long exhale and rose from the chair, following her doctor out of the exam room. With each step forward, feeling like she was in slow motion, each person she passed, looking up and giving her an empathetic look. *Was this really happening, or was this just a bad dream I'm going to wake from?* It all felt so surreal. Exiting the back area, her eyes met Brooks as he quickly rose from the waiting room chair, pushing it back a few inches, causing it to make a cringy scraping sound against the linoleum floor. A sudden tidal wave of emotion rose within her body, and all she managed was a nod as she met his concerned gaze. Within seconds he was there, enveloping her in his arms as she collapsed against him, and the disbelieving tears started to flow.

* * *

"So, your prognosis is good then?" Kolt asked, taking a seat next to her at the kitchen table. He and Jane had returned from their honeymoon early when Georgie got the diagnosis.

"It depends on what type of breast cancer it is actually and what stage it's in. I won't know anything for certain until I speak to the oncologist." Georgie answered, staring into her cup of tea.

"And when is that appointment?" Jane asked, rising from the kitchen table, and setting a sleeping Gatton in his bassinet.

"Tuesday next week."

"And how soon after that will you start treatment?" Kolt asked, his brows knit together as he reached for her hand.

"I have to get my port put in, and then they'll book my first chemo treatment." Georgie answered, meeting his gaze as emotion and guilt started to rise in her chest. "I'm so sorry for interrupting your honeymoon. I don't know how my body will respond to treatment, so I may need to lessen my workload or stop sessions altogether, which is going to affect the business."

"I have some money put away." Her mother said, putting a supportive hand on her shoulder.

"And we can stall breaking ground on our farm site." Kolt said, looking towards Jane, who nodded in agreement.

"You can't do that." Georgie urged, her voice cracking. "You've waited so long to build your farm, and I couldn't live with myself if I took that away from you."

"It's okay, Georgie. We're perfectly happy and content living here for the time being. It doesn't matter if it's delayed." Jane urged; her eyes filled with sincerity.

"We'll do what we need to do as a family to get through this," her mother added, leaning down and planting a kiss on her head. "All you need to concern yourself with right now is getting better."

CHAPTER 7

*P*ulling into his driveway, Brooks smiled when he saw Georgie's SUV parked off to the side of his driveway. She had her oncologist appointment today and had texted asking if she could come over afterwards. As he would be at work till 6 p.m., he told her where to find his spare keys and told her to make herself at home. Climbing the front stairs, he checked the door, which was unlocked, and walked in, immediately being enveloped by the incredible smell of tomatoes, garlic, and savory Italian sausage.

"Honey, I'm home!" he shouted jokingly as he made his way past the staircase to the kitchen. What greeted him was Georgie, dressed only in his large black Johnny Cash T-shirt. The same shirt she wore the night she last slept over. Brooks groaned internally as he took in the scene. With Georgie's back turned, earbuds in her ears, shaking her ass to whatever was playing as she stirred a big pot of noodles on the stove. *I could die a happy man if I came home to this every day.* Brooks leaned against the wall and crossed his ankles and arms over his chest, watching her. Her shoulder-length hair was pulled up in a messy bun, exposing the long expanse of her bare neck, and immediately he itched to trail kisses down that slope of flesh. *So beautiful.*

Turning off the burner, she turned, caught sight of him, and jumped, almost dropping the large wooden spoon she had in her hands. With a giggle, she removed the earbuds as a deep blush rose to her cheeks, already flushed from leaning over the hot stove. "How long were you watching me?"

"Long enough." He answered. "What are you making there?"

"Pasta, lots and lots of pasta." She answered as he rounded the island and joined her in front of the stove, glancing into the saucepans and pots and giving her a nod of approval. "Since I'm starting Chemo next week and apparently it messes with your tastebuds, I figured I'd enjoy all the things I love before everything tastes like shit."

Brooks stared at her, his brow drawing together as he asked, "You start next week?"

"Yep. I have a stage three aggressive, fast-growing form of breast cancer, so they want to get the show on the road as soon as possible." She said so matter-of-factly; it took Brooks aback a little. Seemingly oblivious to his reaction, she turned her attention to the bubbling meat sauce on the stove, gave it a stir and turned off the burner.

Stage three. Fast growing. A barrage of questions filled Brooks' head, but one glance at Georgie told him it wasn't the time or place for a detailed inquiry. Looking at

Georgie right now, here in his kitchen, her face glowing from the steam of the cooked pasta; he sensed from her demeanour that she needed a night to forget or at the very least get distracted. That he could give her.

"It smells amazing," he said, rubbing his hands together. "Anything I can do to help?"

"You can crack open the bottle of wine in the fridge." She answered, turning to him with a masking smile. "Tonight, we celebrate."

Okay. Just go with it. "What are we celebrating, beautiful?"

"Life," she replied simply. "Today we celebrate life."

GEORGIE WAS aware she probably looked and sounded crazy at this moment, the hesitation in Brooks' eyes confirming it. But she wanted to forget tonight. To not think about this raging disease in her body. She wanted to eat, drink, laugh and, despite her years of protest regarding a relationship with Brooks, she wanted him. She hadn't forgotten his declaration to her at Kolt and Jane's wedding. In fact, it had run through her mind on continuous repeat over the past few weeks. Brooks declared he wasn't going to give up on the possibility of them together. Over the course of the past few weeks, he stood beside her, giving her strength as the realization of what she was facing became her reality. So today, as she sat across from her oncologist and she got her official diagnosis, something inexplicable shifted inside her. She was done denying Brooks what he wanted. Life was too short, and it was time to live each day to the fullest. Brooks loved her, desired her and even though she understood her feelings needed a moment to catch up to his, she was going to cross that line with him tonight and cast all her doubts aside. Besides, this might be her last chance to feel the touch of a man before sickness from treatment or the disease itself took over her body and her whole world turned upside down. Who better to give her that chance than Brooks? A man who she cared deeply for and meant the world to her.

Brooks handed her a glass of wine, and she took a sip, leaning against the counter, her eyes trained on him as he moved around his space, her mind reeling and heart beating faster as she considered how to initiate this. *Do I just lean in and kiss him, or do I tell him what I want? Seduce or have a discussion first?*

"Do you mind if I take a shower before we eat?" he asked, meeting her gaze.

"Go ahead." She said, leaning against his counter, biting her bottom lip, and crossing her legs at the ankle, his eyes following the movement, trailing the line of her smooth exposed legs. A combination of confusion and desire, yes that is desire flashed in his eyes as she thought, *I might be overthinking this."*

Brooks's puzzled gaze darted up to hers, and his eyes narrowed. She could almost hear him questioning her intentions. "I'm... going upstairs," he replied hesitantly as he pointed towards the staircase and turned, her eyes following him as he ascended the stairs.

* * *

HOLY SHIT! Brooks felt his cheeks heat as he entered his bedroom. Georgie was acting strangely flirtatious, the way she did when she'd been drinking. The difference: she hadn't been drinking at least not until he handed her that glass of wine. Georgie seemed to be willingly and wantonly coming onto him. It was disconcerting and intriguing but mostly disconcerting. *Why now? Why, after all this time, is she giving me a green light? Is it because of her diagnosis or my declaration?*

Stripping out of his work clothes, he threw them into a hamper and entered his ensuite, climbing into the standing shower. Starting the water, he adjusted it to hot letting the steam fill the room as he stood under the spray, the scalding water running down his body, soothing his aching muscles from his long day at work. Turning, he leaned against the wall, and closed his eyes, the heat pelting his shoulders and providing relief. Suddenly he felt soft hands slide around his middle, causing him to jump and spin around. There in his shower, was Georgie gloriously naked, fully exposed to his roaming gaze, her brown eyes dark with desire and a coquettish smile painted on her beautiful lips.

"What are you doing?" he asked, staggering backwards towards the opposite wall.

"I'm giving you what you want and taking what I want," she replied as she crowded him, her tongue darting out to lick her lips. "I've been thinking about what you said to me at Kolt's wedding. How you feel about me and how you want me. I want you too, Brooks. So much."

Is she really saying this? The woman before him, his every adult fantasy coming true as his arousal stirred at the perfection of her body. A body he wanted so much to touch, but before he took what she was offering, he needed to know. "Georgie, I want you, and you know I always have, but I need to know, is all of this because of what I said or because of the events of the past two weeks? I don't want you to regret this."

Georgie met his gaze, softening at the edges yet still teeming with desire as she lay her hand on his chest and answered, "It's both. The last two weeks have made me realize that life is short, and I would be the one with regrets if I didn't explore this connection between us."

Brooks took in her words and searched her eyes, finding only honesty and sincerity in their depths. She drew closer, skimming her smooth naked body against his, her full peaked breasts brushing his stomach causing his body to respond, all blood rushing south. *This is really happening.* Bringing his hands up to cup her face, he smoothed his thumbs over her eyebrows and down her cheekbones to her full lips. Lips he had dreamed of kissing more times than he could count.

"Can I kiss you?" he asked, searching her face for any shred of doubt.

"Please," she begged, an ache edging her voice.

With one hand threading through her hair, and one hand roaming to the small of her back, he pulled her impossibly closer as he leaned in, lingering just a moment as they shared a breath, then brushed his lips tenderly over hers. A pulse, a heartbeat of awareness, hit him in that moment as her lips molded to his with tender softness. Their mouths moved together tentatively at first, then as they eased into a rhythm, the kiss deepened, and her tongue met his. With hot, sensual exploration, they consumed each other's mouths, tasting, teasing, tangling. Their kiss was hungry and passionate. Breathless, he pulled away trying to catch his breath amidst the thick steam of the hot shower, his head whirling with a million thoughts all at once.

"Georgie, fuck, I want you," he managed, his voice low and deep. "But I don't want to rush this by taking you against the shower wall."

"Maybe I want hot, dirty shower sex," she replied brazenly, sliding her hand over his fully erect member.

"Oh, sweet Jesus!" he exclaimed, sucking in a breath as she stroked him unapologetically. "That feels so good."

"You know what feels better?" She asked, dropping to her knees in front of him as she fisted his length. "This," she answered as she ran her tongue up his shaft, circled the head and dipped the tip of her tongue into the slit at the crown.

With a long-drawn-out moan of pleasure, Brooks gripped desperately at the shower walls, trying to find purchase, his legs shaking to hold himself up as his length disappeared between her lips into her warm wet mouth. Looking down, her eyes lifted to meet his with a wildfire of unbridled passion, mirroring his own as she took him deep again and again. His groans and growls of pleasure echoed through the confined space as she mercilessly teased and toyed with his release.

"Georgie, if you don't stop, I'm going to come down your throat," he growled out as his chest heaved, the sweet burn of his impending orgasm causing his vision to become hazy with pleasure.

But she didn't stop. She just stared up at him, her eyes dark with erotic desire as the burn ignited into a full-blown flame, and he moaned loudly, the sound reverberating against the tile walls. With one more delicious swirl of her tongue over his sensitive crown, his orgasm ricocheted through his body, passing the point of no return. Georgie didn't relent, taking him deep and swallowing every drop he gave her until stars appeared behind his eyelids. Blinking rapidly to focus, his gaze drifted down to where Georgie sat back on her heels, staring up at him, a very satisfied smirk on her face. *Fuck, did that just happen?*

* * *

GEORGIE FELT EMPOWERED as she looked up at Brooks, his face flushed by his orgasm and the heat of the shower, as he tried to catch his breath. She had to admit, the power of having him at her complete mercy was exhilarating. Seeing him like this, naked before her, big, strong, and powerful, towering over her kneeling body, caused an unexpected rush of warmth to cover her skin and her core clenched in anticipation of more.

"That has to be the hottest thing that has ever happened to me," Brooks breathed out as he put out his hand to help her to her feet.

Georgie accepted his hand as he pulled her up, steadying her with his hands on her hips. Hands she had always found so comically large, were now turning her on. She wanted those hands on every part of her, caressing, kneading, massaging her most intimate parts. Pressing the length of her body into him, she brought her hand up to massage between his legs, and he shuddered, letting out a long-drawn-out moan.

"Do you want to touch me? To feel how much you turn me on?" She asked, meeting his lustful gaze as she guided his hand from her hip to between her legs, to where she was wet and pulsed with need. Brooks' gaze turned dark and wanton as his long fingers massaged her folds, finding the sensitive nub and circling it with the pad of his thumb. Wildly aroused, she threw her head back as desire pooled low in her belly. Cradling her body with his other hand, he trailed scorching kisses along the column of her neck.

Raising his head to meet her lust-filled eyes, he said, "Let's take this to the bed." She nodded eagerly as he leaned past her to turn off the shower. Handing her a towel, they dried off quickly. Once dry, Georgie went on her tiptoes, hooking her arms around his neck, and he lifted her, cupping her behind in his large palms as he kissed her hungrily and carried her to his bed. Laying her out, he rose to his full height, a towering oak shadowing her protectively. The expression on his face was one of reverence as his eyes roamed over every curve and dip of her body. The softness of his gaze felt like a sweet caress as he looked his fill. His gaze slowly drifting to her face, their eyes met as he said, "You are so beautiful, Georgie. Just so fucking beautiful."

With a smile, Georgie held out her arms to him as he crawled over her, her legs falling open to make room for his large, powerful body. The intense heat of him hovering over her made her pulse spike as he pressed his hips into hers, his body growing hard again as he lowered his lips to hers in a sensual kiss. *Dear Lord, he can kiss.* The realization made her wonder why they hadn't done this sooner. His lips left hers, blazing a path to the tender skin of her neck, the sensation of his hot kisses and rough brush of his trim beard making goosebumps form on her skin. Looking up to meet her eyes, he said. "I don't want to hurt you in any way, so please tell me if I do, okay?"

"Don't touch my left side; my underarm and breast are sensitive." she replied, breathless. "The other side is okay."

Nodding, he placed tender kisses down her neck and along her collarbone. She closed her eyes, getting lost in the onslaught of sensation as he circled her right nipple with his tongue and drew it into his mouth.

"Ah, that feels so good," she cried out, bowing her back off the bed as he sucked her in deep then released the bud with a pop before he soothed it with his tongue. Navigating south, he painted her stomach with hot, scorching kisses, his tongue dipped into her belly button, then trailed down to her sex. Before she realized what he was doing, his face was at her core, his large palms splayed on either side of her thighs, spreading her wide. She glanced down at him, his dark blue eyes locked on hers as he languidly ran his tongue along her seam, circling her button of pleasure. "Brooks...oh!" she gasped loudly, as he feasted on her centre, the scruff of his beard against her thighs and sensitive flesh adding to the glorious sensations. Shamelessly, she writhed under his relentless attention, as he nipped, licked, circled, each sweep and flick of his tongue bringing her higher to a place no one had ever taken her before. It wasn't the first time she had oral sex, but never had it felt like this. Like he was a starving man and only she could satisfy his hunger. Feeling the sweet sensation of her climax cresting, she reached for his hair, curling her fingers around the strands as she rocked into his face, greedily seeking more friction. As if reading her mind, he circled her sensitive nub with the pad of his thumb as he inserted a long digit inside her heat, crooking ever so slightly to massage that perfect spot inside her channel causing her to tip over the edge. A crashing wave of pleasure rolled through her, and she surrendered to the ecstasy of letting go. As she came down from the high, a warm flush covered her body as delicious tingles kissed her skin, and she opened her eyes to see Brooks, kissing up her body, as his intense eyes met hers so much love and devotion in his gaze.

As was their usual modus operandi, she wanted to say something silly, like "good job" or "thanks for the stellar orgasm". Perhaps offer him a high five, but her response caught in her throat, and emotion rose in her chest. Her heart swelled as she stared into his baby blues as if seeing him for the first time. Truly, honestly seeing the man who had been with her through thick and thin, every high and low of life and whom she knew would be by her side through what she could only assume would be a time that would test her strength and resolve. Brooks was so much more than her best friend; Brooks Isley was the love of her life. The realization of this sent an inexplicably euphoric feeling to wash over her, and she couldn't live another moment on this earth without saying those reverent words.

"I love you, Brooks," she declared on an exhale. "I love you. I don't know why I never realized it before, but I think I've always loved you; I was just scared that I would lose you if we crossed that line. I don't ever want to lose you." She croaked out, emotion breaking her voice and making her throat ache as she swallowed back the tears. "My life doesn't make sense without you in it."

"I'm not going anywhere, Georgie. I love you too, so much." He declared as he brushed his lips gently to hers. "All I want and need is you."

"Make love to me, Brooks," she breathed out, overcome by this wave of love, emotion and unbridled desire that was consuming her and swallowing her whole. "I need you."

Leaning over her, he opened his nightstand, produced a condom, and sat back on his heels, his eyes never leaving hers as he ripped the package open and sheathed himself. Climbing back over her, she lifted her legs higher as he pressed his hips into her, his hard length finding her entrance ready for him. As he entered her, her body opened for him, drawing him deeper than anyone had ever been. Filling an empty space within her that yearned for this raw emotional connection. The feeling of fullness felt new and sweet, and the desire to move, to feel that exquisite friction, was overpowering. Fully seated inside her, she brushed the stray curls from his eyes and cupped his face, pulling him in for a sensuous kiss. As they kissed, his hips started to move, slowly sliding in and out of her body. She met each thrust with her hips, the drag and press igniting a simmering fire inside her belly.

"If I'm dreaming, never wake me," he breathed out against her lips as he kissed her long and deep.

"It's real. This... is... real," she managed, the sheer pleasure of him inside her making her words come out in short, breathless bursts. The heat of his strong, heavy body on top of her as he pressed her into the mattress added to the heady, mind-bending power of their connection, and she felt lost to all the new sensations he was producing within her. "It's never felt this good," she said in a long-drawn-out moan as she bit his shoulder lightly.

"It's so perfect," he replied as he suddenly flipped her, inverting their position, still connected with her on top. "Ride me, Beautiful. I want to see all of you."

Finding her momentum, she ground into him with each press and perfect slide of his length buried deep inside her body. With his large hands on her hips, he encouraged her movements over him, meeting her rhythm, yet giving her complete control. Taking control like this made her feel strong and powerful, and she needed that. So much in her life seemed out of her control right now, and in this moment, he was giving her this. Giving her something she so desperately needed. Picking up her pace, she threw her head back as her orgasm coiled tighter and with one more rock and grind of her hips it let go. That sweet burn of sensation filled her body again as the fire of pleasure rolled through her, and she stilled, Brooks bending his knees to take over by thrusting into her from underneath. She opened her eyes to meet his as he pressed deep and shattered beneath her. Her inner muscles milked every ounce of pleasure from him as he let out a strangled growl. Their eyes met, satiated with pleasure, and overflowing with love. And in that moment Georgie knew, that this was it. Brooks Isley was the one she had been waiting for.

* * *

BROOKS WASN'T sure what he did in this lifetime to deserve this blissful feeling but laying there in his bed with Georgie's naked, sexy body wrapped around him like a spider monkey clinging to a tree, made him think he must have done something pretty darn good. After they had both come down from the high of their orgasms, they simply lay there in reverent silence, relishing the feel of being in each other's arms. He had dreamt of this more times than he could count, but never could he have imagined how impossibly good it would feel. Not only physically but also emotionally. She had declared her love for him, his unrequited feelings now reciprocated, and that alone was more than he could have hoped or dreamed for. Georgie shifted, resting her chin on his chest as her satiated gaze settled on his.

"What are you thinking?" she asked, a satisfied smile curling her lips.

"I'm thinking I love you, of course. And I'm thinking, hot damn, we set these sheets on fire!" he exclaimed with a waggle of his eyebrows.

Georgie let out a raspy giggle as she added, "I don't mean to brag, but I think we kind of rocked the whole sex thing."

"Hell, yeah, we did!" he exclaimed as he pulled her in for a hungry kiss. She pulled her lips away breathless, and Brooks' stomach took that moment to rumble.

"Dinner!" Georgie exclaimed as she steamrolled over Brooks and climbed out of bed. His eyes appreciating her in all her naked glory, she strode over to where she'd shed his t-shirt and slipped it back on. "I completely forgot about it."

Brooks watched as she sauntered over to the bedroom door, opened it, and looked over her shoulder, meeting his gaze as she said in a sultry voice, "Are you joining me, big guy?"

Big guy. Brooks didn't need to be asked twice. Rolling out of bed, he stalked over to her, making her squeal with delight as he chased her down the stairs in nothing but his birthday suit. Swooping her into his arms, he threw her over his shoulder and carried her caveman style into the kitchen. Setting her down on the counter, she crossed her legs and playfully bit her lip as she watched him fire up the oven burner.

"You know, cooking naked is kind of dangerous. I wouldn't want you to damage anything important." She commented with a coy smile, her eyes roaming admiringly over his body. Brooks turned, looking down at his bare body and strode over to the corner pantry where he produced a BBQ apron that said 'Caution Extremely Hot' eliciting a hysterical laugh from Georgie.

Fastening it behind his back, he assumed a warrior pose and asked, "Better?"

"Much," she replied as he turned, exposing his naked butt, and giving her a little wiggle. Georgie burst into a fit of giggles as his heart swelled at his favorite sound in the entire world.

Warming up the pasta, he plated them both a portion, and they made their way over to the living room, settling in on the couch. Flicking on the TV, he flipped through channels until Georgie nodded, deciding on a rerun of "Friends".

Georgie curled up next to him, her head resting on his shoulder while they ate. They ate slowly, savoring not only the delicious meal she made but the delicious feeling of being this intimate. Before long, her eyelids drooped, and Georgie met his gaze with an exhausted look. "Are you tired, Beautiful?" he asked, his brows drawing together in concern as he took her plate from her hands.

"So tired." She replied as she shifted herself so she could lay her head on his lap. "I'm just going to rest here a while." Within minutes Georgie was asleep, her sweet snore sounding over the noise of the TV.

Muting the show with the remote, Brooks set his plate down on the side table and glanced down at Georgie, brushing her unruly damp hair from her eyes, marveling at her beautiful angelic face. A flood of memories washed over him as he remembered watching her sleep for the first time. They had been camping in the backyard, both huddled in the tent, in their respective sleeping bags. The light had dawned, and the inside of the orange nylon tent glowed as the sun was starting to rise through the thin material. It cast a glow on her face, and in that moment, he thought, *this is what an angel looks like.* Georgie was his angel then and his angel now.

A painful lump of emotion formed in his throat as her earlier words echoed at the edge of his consciousness. *Stage three. An aggressive, fast-growing form of cancer.* Hot tears started to well up in his eyes, and he glanced down at her so peacefully sleeping, as the realization that this thing, this horrible disease, was slowly attacking her. He felt a restrained sob reverberate up his throat, and he gulped it back, trying desperately not to cry. Georgie needed him to be strong, to be her mighty oak standing beside her and keeping her grounded to this earth. And yet, here in this quiet moment with her fast asleep on his lap, all he could do was make a silent plea to the heavens not to take his angel away.

* * *

"I'm going to move in with Brooks for a while," Georgie announced over breakfast. Around the table, everyone's eyes instantly turned to her, their shock evident as she dunked her teabag into the hot water in her mug.

"Why would you do that?" her mother asked, her face etched with a mix of confusion and concern. "You start chemo next week, and with Kolt and Jane back, I'll be able to plan the horse camps around your treatments."

"I know, Mom, and thank you for that, but I really want Brooks to take me, and I promise I'll call if I need you." She replied, giving her mother a reassuring smile.

Kolt gave her a puzzled look as he picked up his coffee cup. "Is there something more that you aren't telling us here about you and Brooks?"

Georgie rolled her eyes at her brother conceding, "Okay fine, you were all right about Brooks and me. Brooks and I are dating."

"Finally!" Kolt exclaimed, getting up from the table, reaching for Jane's empty plate and stacking it with his as she fed Gatton. "It's about time you gave that poor guy a chance."

Her mother was silent but gave her a wary look as she leaned against the counter and lifted her mug of coffee to her lips. Georgie spotted it immediately, rose from the table and turned to face her mother with her hand on her hip. "Do you have something to say?"

Setting her coffee cup down, she met her daughter's gaze as she replied, "You know I've always been Team Brooks, but you've been through a lot in a short period of time and well, this all seems a little sudden and impulsive." Her mother chimed in. "I know you've been friends with that boy for a long time, but you've never given any indication of wanting to date him, despite our coaxing and teasing. He's so loyal to you, and you have the potential to break his heart if you don't feel the same as he does. Brooks wants marriage, kids, the white picket fence, and although I realize you want those things too, you need to ask yourself if you want those things with Brooks. Especially now that you have no choice but to put your future on hold."

Georgie stood there speechless, utterly speechless that her mother had the audacity to say all of that to her. *Does she really think so little of me that she's concerned that I'm simply toying with Brooks emotions? That I'm only in this relationship with him because I'm sick and there is no one else. This is why I need to move in with Brooks. This is why I need to get out of this house.*

"Thanks, Mom, for always being the buzzkill." Georgie said as she set her mug down in the sink, turning towards the stairs. Climbing the first few steps, she turned and shot a glare at her mother. "Did you ever stop to think that maybe being diagnosed with cancer has forced me to finally see what is good in my life and if God forbid, I lose this battle at least I got to know what it's like to be loved..." she said her voice trembling and her eyes welling up with tears as she added, "...and love someone in return."

"Georgie...I..." her mother started, her eyes wide with regret and surprise at her confession.

"That's fine, Mom," Georgie said, holding up her hand and then turning to ascend the stairs. "It's good I finally know what you think of me. I'm going to go pack my things."

GEORGIE WAS FUMING as she pulled clothes out of her dresser and threw them on the bed. She was making a mess of her otherwise organized packing, but she was furious. So angry that her mother took this opportunity to voice her opinion on her new relationship with Brooks. So incredibly angry that she thought so little of her that she even considered that Georgie was taking advantage of Brooks affections. Bottom line, she deserved to be happy, and Brooks made her happy.

A knock sounded at her door, and she hesitated, hoping it wasn't her mother. The last person she wanted to talk to was her.

"Georgie, it's me, open up." Kolt's voice sounded on the other side of the door.

Georgie strode over to the door and pressed the knob in to unlock it. Kolt opened the door and peered in, his eyes going to the askew pile of clothes on her bed. Opening the door further, he strode in, two large suitcases in his hands, and set them down beside her. "Thought you might need these," he said quietly, pushing aside some of the clothes and taking a seat on the corner of the bed. "Do you need some help?"

"I can manage." She replied, reaching for a suitcase, setting it on the bed and unzipping it.

Kolt sat for a few minutes watching her toss clothes from her closet into the suitcase before he commented. "That was pretty intense down there. Mom was out of line."

"You think?" Georgie questioned sarcastically as she stepped out of her closest and put her hands on her hips. "She basically said I was playing Brooks for a fool. Just messing with him like it was some kind of game."

Kolt ran his hands through his hair nervously. "I'm sure she didn't mean it the way it came out. She's just concerned about you, Georgie."

"Are you defending her?" Georgie asked, squinting her eyes at Kolt. "Because if you are, there's the door." She added, gesturing towards her bedroom door.

"No, no, nothing like that," he said, shaking his head. "I'm all for you and Brooks finally getting your shit together. And truly, Jane and I are incredibly happy for you both, but you must understand where Mom's head is right now. Her daughter has been diagnosed with stage three breast cancer, a rare and aggressive form no less, and she's scared. She's scared of losing you, Georgie. Both actually and figuratively."

Georgie softened her stance a moment, the tension in her shoulders easing with his words. "I'm scared too, and I'm the one having to face all of this."

"And that's why I'm not defending her, just asking you to understand where she's coming from, and perhaps give her a bit of grace," he said as he stood from the bed and made his way to the door. "Let me know when you're all packed and I'll help you carry your bags out to your vehicle."

"I appreciate that." Georgie said, meeting his gaze.

Kolt opened the door and turned his eyes, meeting hers, and his lips curled up in a knowing smile as he asked, "Feels good to be in love, doesn't it?"

"So good." Georgie choked out as she watched her brother turn and walk out the door.

CHAPTER 8

Their relationship was full steam ahead, and Brooks was here for it. It had been four days since he and Georgie had crossed the proverbial line between friends to lovers, and in that time she had moved herself in, had given him no less than twelve spectacular orgasms and had fit herself seamlessly into his daily life. Watching her curled up on his couch eating popcorn as she watched *Sixteen Candles* for the millionth time, he couldn't help but marvel at how stunning she was. Even in his old Johnny Cash T-shirt he was certain now he was never getting back, a pair of fluffy bright yellow slipper socks and her hair wet and pulled up into a messy topknot with a rainbow scrunchie after yet another indecently erotic shower. Georgie was breathtaking.

Leaning against the cased opening of his living room, in just a pair of flannel pajama bottoms, he watched as she tossed a handful of popcorn into her mouth and giggled as Molly Ringwald gasped in horror at Anthony Michael

Hall's request for her underpants. Letting out a chuckle of his own, her eyes darted up to meet his, and her lips curled up into a coy smile.

"Are you going to join me, Big Guy?" she asked, wiggling her eyebrows at him. Her new term of endearment for him, surprisingly arousing. Stalking over to the couch, she squealed as he lifted her and set her on his lap, nuzzling her neck with his bearded chin and growling as he grazed her earlobe with his teeth. "Brooks," she protested on a moan as he kissed down the column of her neck. "I'm missing my movie."

"Spoiler alert, he sleeps with the popular chick," he replied, nipping her earlobe again. "Can we now get to the chill part of Netflix and chill?"

Georgie laughed as she rose from his lap and leaned over, setting down the popcorn bowl on the coffee table, and glanced at him coquettishly over her shoulder. He groaned as he noticed she hadn't bothered to put on any underwear. Turning to look at him, she lifted his shirt over her head, and a low rumbly growl of appreciation reverberated up his throat. Her body was lean, toned, and curvaceous in all the right places, and seeing her like this so bold and brazen was never going to get old. As his eyes roamed the expanse of her skin, his gaze inadvertently flitted to where the skin was darker, scarred from her healed biopsy, and he quickly brought his eyes back to hers. In an instant, her face fell as she reached for the discarded t-shirt and started to put it back on. Brooks grabbed her wrist, stopping her, meeting the rush of sadness in her eyes. Without saying a word, he sat up, pulled her closer, his hands on her waist, and planted a tender kiss on the scar. Eyes drifting back to hers, a world of emotion reflecting back at him, she cupped his face and leaned in, brushing her lips to his. The kiss started out delicate, soft and as the passion between them quelled, it deepened into something searching, seeking, for the comfort they could only find with each other. Rising from his lap, she hooked her fingers into the side of his pajama pants, Brooks lifting himself to help her remove them along with his underwear.

"There's a condom in my pocket," he said roughly as he watched her retrieve it, open it, and sheath him, her eyes never leaving his. Expecting her to climb back on his lap and straddle him, instead she turned and straddled him in reverse, rising so he could sink into her scorching heat. She rolled her hips, gyrating slowly, sensually, over him, the position creating an erotic and delicious friction as she took what she needed. Bringing his hand to her breast, he kneaded it gently, then paused as he asked, "Is this okay?"

"Yes", she replied as he rolled her nipple between his fingers, as he held onto her hip with his other hand, and she bowed her back off his chest with a gasp and a long feral moan. Sliding his hand down her smooth stomach to her wet heat, his fingers brushed her centre, and she cried out, breathless and raw with need. "There, yes, touch me there." His fingers pressed, circled the sensitive nub until she was shaking and pulsing under his touch.

"That's it, beautiful," he murmured into her ear, feeling his own release on the horizon, her throaty sounds making him so unspeakably aroused. With Georgie shamelessly writhing on top of him, he increased his pace as he sucked in her earlobe, and she shattered, her internal muscles rippling and clenching around him as her pleasure took her under. Her release ratcheted his own he followed her as they slowly rode out the wave. Both panting, he wrapped his arms around her waist protectively, and she clung to him, neither of them wanting to let go.

That night as they lay in bed, the full moon outside casting a soft glow in the room, Georgie curled into the groove of his body and whispered, "I'm scared."

His throat constricted painfully with her words, and he swallowed hard. They had always been forthright with each other, and right now there were no words adequate enough to take away that fear. What she was about to enter into was the unknown. There were no promises as to the outcome and no trapdoors to escape. Not for her, not for him and certainly not for them. All he could do was to share in her fear, so she knew she wasn't alone. Swallowing back the overwhelming emotion, he replied, "I'm scared too, Georgie."

LOOKING IN THE MIRROR, Georgie touched the raised skin just above her breastbone that housed her chemotherapy port and sighed. *Another ugly scar.*

Brooks entered the ensuite, curly hair askew and looking sexily rumpled from sleep. He wrapped his arms around her waist and kissed her neck, meeting her eyes in the mirror. They had lived together for three weeks, and

Brooks in the morning had to be her favorite. He was so adorably disheveled, and she would always find herself wondering why she had fought her feelings for him for so long.

"Good morning, Big Guy," she said, turning to meet his gaze and sliding her hands around his waist. "Are you ready for this?"

"I should ask you that question." he volleyed back, searching her eyes.

"I mean, as ready as I'll ever be, I guess," she replied, looking down at her port.

He nodded, and a small smirk curved up his lips. "Do you know why portholes on ships are round?" Blurting out a giggle, she shook her head, her smile growing wider. "So, when you open one to look out, a wave won't hit you square in the face."

Georgie rolled her eyes, giving him a swat on the arm, then wrapping herself around him in a hug. She buried her face in his chest, grateful for the comic relief on this sure to be heavy day.

* * *

GEORGIE AND BROOKS checked into the Cancer Treatment Centre in St. Augustine. The place was bright with large windows, but sterile with that distinct over-sanitized hospital smell. A nurse led her to a vinyl chair, where she was told to take a seat. There were two other patients there: a middle-aged woman wearing a brightly colored cap, a book in her hand, and an older man who looked like he was fast asleep. The nurse went through her treatment, the course of drugs she would be given over the next four hours, and generally explained what to expect both during and after the treatment. She glanced at Brooks, diligently taking notes on a little notepad, and asking questions. Georgie smiled, so grateful to have him with her this first time. He gave her a wink as the nurse attached her IV to her port, and once it started, the nurse brought her a blanket and Brooks a chair so he could sit with her.

"Since we have to be here for four hours, I brought some things with me to help you get through this," he said, lifting a backpack she must have been too distracted to notice. "This Georgette Donahue is your chemo survival pack." Georgie grinned as she watched him unzip the backpack. "In here, I have some fun things to help distract you." Digging into the bag, he pulled out a romance novel with a classic shirtless man, with hair that cascaded in the wind, kissing the neck of a beautiful woman, and Georgie laughed. "Not sure if it's as hot as Reggie and Mim's story, but the lady at the drugstore highly recommended it," he informed with a waggle of his eyebrows as he handed it to her then continued his exploration of the bag. Pulling out a worse for wear stuffed horse, she recognized it as one she had when she was younger. She glanced up at him, meeting his eyes and wondering where he got it from. "I brought this little fella because I remember you and he were inseparable growing up and he always brought you comfort, so I figured now was as good a time as any for a reunion."

"Thank you, Brooks, that's so sweet." She said, taking the stuffed toy from him and holding it close to her chest.

"Oh, I'm not done yet, Beautiful" he replied with a huge smile and an adorable wink.

Brooks proceeded to pull out a pink toque and slippers that both said, "Kicking Cancer's Ass", a notebook which he coyly said she could use to write him sexy notes. A deck of cards just so they could hone their poker game in case they had an opportunity to win it all in Vegas. A tablet on which he downloaded her favorite movies, including "Sixteen Candles," and his old iPod with earphones that still held all their favorite songs from when they were 12. As she clutched her favorite stuffed horse, she gazed at him, feeling so much love and gratitude.

"What do you want to do first?" he asked eagerly, rubbing his hands together.

"Poker, of course." She replied with a mischievous smirk, and he nodded in approval of her apt choice.

* * *

BROOKS HELD Georgie's hair back as she heaved into the toilet bowl. She had been fine when they got home, surprisingly energetic, but as soon as she smelled the stir-fry he made her, full of healthy veggies and lean protein, she felt nauseous. She leaned back on her heels, and he handed her a towel to wipe her mouth.

"I think I'm okay now." She said, wobbling to her feet like a baby horse trying to walk for the first time.

"Here, take these," he said, handing her some anti-nausea pills the nurse had given them. "The nurse said they would help."

She did as he requested, swallowing them with water tentatively as she leaned against him, her body now weak.

"Let's get you into bed, beautiful." He suggested as he lifted her into his arms and carried her up the stairs to their bedroom.

"But dinner." She protested, meeting his gaze with half-hooded eyes.

"You can warm it up later if you feel up to eating," he said, kissing her head as she clung to him and he pulled back the covers, setting her on the cool sheets.

"Will you stay with me for a while? Maybe read to me?" she asked, her tired, melting chocolate eyes begging him.

"Of course. What do you want me to read?"

"The bodice ripper would be fine." She said with a grin.

"Alright now, let me go grab it from downstairs," he said with a laugh, jogging out of the room and down the stairs to retrieve the book from her survival pack. Returning to the bedroom with the book in hand, he approached the bed to find Georgie asleep.

He smiled and set the book down on the end table, leaning in to plant a kiss on her cheek. Setting a garbage can near the bed, he flicked off the light and heard a knock at the front door. Closing the bedroom door, he made his way down the stairs and opened the front door to find Emmaline Donahue standing there. She had two large canvas coolers next to her, and the look on her face was a combination of uncertainty and regret.

"Mrs. Donahue," he said, surprised. "Come on in," he

offered, stepping aside so she could come into the front entrance.

"The ladies auxiliary wanted to help, so they made you and Georgie some healthy meals," she said, looking down at the bags next to her.

"That's so nice," he replied, gesturing her inside as he stepped out onto the porch to retrieve the cooler bags.

"They can be frozen so you can take them out whenever you need them." She said, her voice tinged with trepidation as she asked, "Is Georgie here?"

"She's asleep upstairs. As you know, her first treatment was today." He said, guiding her down the hall to the kitchen, still a mess from his abandoned meal for Georgie.

"Oh," she responded with surprise, which made him turn and furrow his brows.

"You didn't know?" he asked, setting down the cooler bags on the kitchen table.

"No," she replied, her eyes going downcast, emotion edging her voice. "Georgie hasn't talked to me since the day she moved in here."

That was news to Brooks. Georgie and her mother were close, but he had no idea they weren't talking. He understood they butted heads sometimes, but shutting her out completely wasn't something Georgie would do, and he had a feeling Mrs. Donahue was hoping to talk to her, perhaps clear the air. Brooks understood with her here now in his house, he would have to be the sounding board.

"Would you like a cup of tea?" he asked, gesturing to the kettle.

"Yes, that would be nice, dear," she replied as she took

a seat at the kitchen table. Starting the kettle, Brooks retrieved two mugs from the cupboard and pulled out an assortment of tea. Setting everything down on the table with a bowl of sugar and honey, which was Georgie's favorite, he took a seat across from Mrs. Donahue. Meeting her wary gaze, she asked, "How was Georgie's first treatment?"

"Good. She was a trooper. I stayed with her throughout the whole thing, keeping her laughing and distracted. Just trying to keep her positive."

Emmaline Donahue smiled, resting her hands on the warm mug in front of her. "You've always had a way of brightening things for her. When she would get down about something or be anxious, you would always make her laugh and lift her spirits."

"She does that for me too," he replied. "I can't imagine my life without her."

Emmaline's eyes welled up with tears as she met his. "You love her, don't you?"

"More than anything," he replied. "And she loves me too."

"I realize that now," she replied, her comment surprising him. "I doubted my daughter's intentions with you in the beginning, and I voiced it. Not wanting either of you to get hurt. But what I have now come to realize is that Georgie has always loved you, Brooks. She has always compared every man she has dated to you. You were the benchmark."

Brooks smiled and met her eyes. "I did the same thing as there has only ever been Georgie for me."

Emmaline's smile deepened at that as she raised her

mug to take a sip of her tea and set it down with a soft laugh. "Did your mother ever tell you that she and I have been secretly planning your wedding for years?"

"No, why you two sneaky matchmakers!" he exclaimed, sitting back in his chair. "Why am I not surprised?"

CHAPTER 9

Georgie was feeling surprisingly good after her first two treatments and, despite some nausea right after each one, she felt well enough to take on a few therapy sessions. After Brooks informed Georgie of her mother's impromptu visit, they had spoken several times and things between them were on the mend. Regardless, there was no way she was moving back into the farmhouse. Living with Brooks had been incredible, and with her third round of chemo fast approaching, there was nowhere else she wanted to be.

Kolt walked out of the office, a sling wrapped around his body, with baby Gatton cradled inside. Georgie laughed when she saw him, so different from the man she knew only a year ago. "Mr. Mom. Look at you all domesticated." She teased, peeling back the sling to reveal a happy baby staring up at her with his big brown eyes.

"Jane was finally feeling up for a ride, so she and Prairie are in the east field while I take care of this little guy," he said, planting a kiss on Gatton's blonde head before he brought his gaze back to Georgie. "Nice to see you back here."

"Yeah, I missed my clients, and although they've been understanding, I still want to try to do some sessions when I feel up to it," she said. "I have my third treatment in a few days, and they say it gets progressively worse as they go."

Kolt nodded his head and then smirked. "I saw Brooks the other day. Bumped into him at the Eazy and well, I don't think I've seen him happier. If a man could glow, that man was glowing."

Georgie laughed, sliding her hands into her back pockets, and kicking a piece of gravel with her boot. "That's what regular sex does for you."

"Whoa! TMI, I don't want to know!" Kolt exclaimed, putting his hands up and shaking his head.

Georgie laughed, loving to tease her brother at any opportunity until her expression turned serious. "Honestly, I'm scared this is all going to end up being too much for him." She confessed, her smile turning to a frown. "It's only going to get harder from here."

"Don't you think you should let Brooks decide that? I know that Brooks would follow you to the ends of the earth if you asked him to." Kolt said. "You need to trust that he's got this."

"I know, there's just so many unknowns."

"But isn't that life?" Kolt shrugged. "Life is never guaranteed. That's why you need to make the most of every moment. Look at Jane and me. Once we stopped worrying about what could happen and started living, our relationship grew tenfold and strengthened into something solid and unbreakable.

Georgie considered Kolt's words for a moment. He was right; she needed to live each day as if it was her last while she still could. Smiling, an idea formulated in her head as to how she was going to do just that starting tonight.

DRIVING NORTH, Brooks reached for Georgie's hand as they pulled into a small resort town on Lake Winnipeg. When he came home from work, she had surprised him with packed suitcases and plans for a weekend getaway. Two nights at a lakeside resort, dinners out and walks along the boardwalk and beach. A perfect way to spend the weekend with his girl.

With another treatment on Monday, it was not lost on either of them that they needed this little escape before reality came back to slap them in the face. Two treatments in and Georgie had been feeling good, but both understood that it was simply the calm before the storm.

Finding the resort, they checked in quickly and found their room, a large suite with a living space and a separate bedroom with a king-size bed divided by wood and glass doors. The furnishings were soft and comfortable, and the main living space led out to a balcony with a view of the lake, beach, boardwalk, and harbor. Georgie opened the patio door. The late August breeze off the water was cool and damp in the light of the fading sun. Stars were just starting to appear in the darkening sky over the lake expanse. Hearing a stir behind her, Georgie glanced back and smiled as Brooks joined her on the balcony and wrapped his arms around her, encapsulating her in his warmth.

"This was a good idea," he said, nuzzling his chin into the crook of her neck. "We needed this."

"Agreed," she replied, turning in his arms, and backing him through the open patio door into the suite, a playful twinkle in her eyes. "Why don't we strip down, climb into those cozy robes hanging on the back of the bathroom door and order in pizza?"

"A naughty pizza party, yes please," he replied, making Georgie giggle as he set to work ordering their dinner. Watching her strip out of her clothes, so comfortable in her body as she walked around the bedroom, gloriously naked and bold, he smiled. Having known Georgie so long, he never would have guessed her to be so unapolo-getically sexual, but her voracious appetite for him was both a wonder and a surprise. It made him want to do and try everything with her. To explore every facet of this newfound intimacy between them. And in the short time that they had taken their relationship to the physical level, they had made quite a dent in that amorous list.

The reality was, though, that Georgie was going to get sicker, and treatment would likely extinguish some of her sexual desire. As spoiled as he was now, he needed to be okay with that. Even though the sex between them so far had been mind blowing and incredible, if all she was able to offer him was the touch of her hand on his, a simple hug, a sweet kiss or even her beautiful smile, he would be happy. All he needed was her, in whatever capacity she was able.

With their pizza on the way, he set down his phone and started unbuttoning his shirt as his eyes zoned in on Georgie's from across the room and a coy smirk painted his lips. "How about we skip the robes and stay naked all weekend?" he asked, dropping his jeans and kicking them off as he stalked over to her and swept her into his arms, making her squeal. Laying her out on the bed, he crawled over her, kneeling between her legs, his eyes feasting on her body as he lowered his mouth to her stomach nibbled the tender flesh and branded a trail of hot kisses up her body to capture her mouth. Kissing her deeply passionately, their tongues tangled in a torrid embrace. Brooks wanted to consume her, his lips hungry and seeking, wanting more. Breathless, he lifted his head, her chocolate eyes hazy puddles of lust.

A knock on the door startled them both, and he groaned as he kissed her chastely and crawled off the bed, reaching for a robe and making her laugh as he realized it barely wrapped around him. Chuckling too, he went with it as another knock sounded and he jogged to the door. Paying for their pizza, he returned with two bottled waters and a large pizza box to find Georgie sitting crisscross on the bed with a robe wrapped around her. Setting the pizza in the middle of the bed, she flipped it open, and grabbed a slice not waiting for Brooks to find plates and napkins. Taking a bite, she moaned and nodded her head. Brooks laughed, joining her on the bed as he grabbed a slice for himself. Watching Georgie so happy and carefree, something had been on his mind since she sprang this impromptu trip on him, and he needed to know.

"What made you want to get away this weekend?" he asked. "I mean, it's not like you to be spontaneous like this."

Georgie set down her pizza slice and reached for the napkin Brooks had set in front of her. "I was talking to Kolt today, and well, he reminded me that it's important to live in the here and now, taking advantage of every moment. I guess I realized I wasted too many moments that I could have been loving you." She said, meeting his gaze, then offering him a wistful smile added, "You know if I would've put away my fears of losing or complicating our friendship aside and just trusted that you were the one meant for me, you and I could've been married and have had kids by now."

"Do you still want that? The marriage and a family, with me?" he asked, searching her eyes.

"I do more than anything." She replied, with an ache in her voice as her mouth settled into a resolute line. "But I don't know if I'll be able to give you that. My future seems so uncertain right now."

Brooks closed the pizza box and set it aside, pulling her onto his lap, facing him. "Georgie, you're going to fight this, and you're going to win this battle. I know you, Georgie Donahue; you never give up. And as for marriage, I'm ready whenever you are. You just tell me when and where and whatever comes afterwards; we'll figure it out together."

Georgie bit her bottom lip, her eyebrow raising as she clarified, "When and where?"

"When and where," he echoed, meeting her gaze.

"How about two weeks from now at Prairie Charm Bed and Breakfast?"

Stunned, Brooks blinked, and a slow smile curled his lips. "I'll talk to Falyn and see what she can do." He said, wrapping her in a hug and letting out a deep joyous laugh. "I haven't even formally asked, and I don't have a ring. This is crazy!"

"I don't need a ring. All I need is you, Brooks. I love you so much, so ask me already!" she exclaimed with a giggle, pushing him back on the bed and climbing over him.

"Georgette Donahue, will you marry me?" he asked as she hovered over him, their lips mere inches apart.

"Yes," she replied, kissing him chastely.

"Oh, my God, I love you!" he said, rolling them and pinning her to the mattress. "You're going to be my wife."

"And you're going to be my husband." She whispered as she kissed him tenderly, reverently sealing her promise to him. Brooks had never felt so happy in his entire life.

* * *

BY THE TIME they were home on Sunday, Falyn's bed-and-breakfast had been booked, and her mother had arranged for Savanah Perez, Primrose's guru of wedding planning, to put together the event. Soon their quiet weekend turned into a continuous barrage of calls and texts from family and friends, congratulating them and asking what they could do. Finally, turning off their cell phones, they walked the pier, taking in the colorful mosaics painted on the concrete walls, watching as sailboats either left the port for a sunset run or docked for the night. They walked to the end by the lighthouse and found a perch on a large rock watching the sunset. It was an evening Georgie would hold on to the memory of as her once safe and certain world began to spiral out of control.

CHAPTER 10

Georgie's body was on fire, the warm flush of the chemo drugs burning her from the inside out. Perspiration coated her body like a second skin, yet she was so cold it felt like she had plunged into frigid water, pins and needles attacking her body. Glancing at the clock, she knew Brooks would be home any minute. But she couldn't wait, the need to get help consuming her. *Something is wrong. This isn't normal.* She stood from the couch, hunched over, using the coffee table to inch herself closer to the cased opening that led to the kitchen. With sharp, stilted breaths, she straightened to stand fully, her entire body in flames and her knees feeling like they were going to give out. Managing to steady herself, she took a tiny step forward, followed by another and another, reaching out for the wall to lean on. *But am I touching the wall? I can't feel my fingers.* She groaned, her head spinning. *Why did you leave your phone in the kitchen?* Leaving behind the safety of the wall, she stepped forward, trying to concentrate on putting one foot in front of the next as she inched excruciatingly closer to the kitchen island where her phone sat. Suddenly her vision blurred, everything going out of focus as the room spun and the hard floor connected with her head.

* * *

HOT TEARS STUNG Brooks's eyes as he sat by Georgie's bedside. Bea Smithfield, a fellow Primrose resident and Emergency Room nurse came in, offering him a compassionate smile as she changed Georgie's IV bag. Brooks knew Bea well and was grateful to have a familiar face taking care of his Georgie. Setting a supportive hand on his shoulder, Bea met his gaze. "She'll wake up soon, Brooks," before she exited the room.

Brooks closed his eyes, his mind immediately reliving the scariest moment of his life. Georgie passed out on the kitchen floor when he came home from work. The anguished cry that escaped his mouth as he rushed to her side, quickly feeling for a pulse, and when he found one, calling 911 with trembling hands. The sound of the ambulance, the paramedics rushing in to assess her, finding her unresponsive but breathing and carefully lifting her onto a gurney. The drive. The excruciatingly long drive to the hospital, trying to keep up with the ambulance as he prayed over and over that Georgie would be okay. He was spent, emotionally exhausted, sitting here, waiting for her to wake, one hand holding hers and one hand tugging at his hair.

When they arrived at the hospital, they found out she was running a high fever, a symptom of her chemo treatment, and was severely dehydrated. Georgie had spent the last few days saying water tasted metallic, but never did he think that she hadn't been hydrating herself. He shook his head, feeling more tears wanting to escape, setting his head down and resting it on the hospital bed mattress as he held her limp hand. It had been hours, how many he wasn't sure, but he couldn't let go of her hand, scared that if he did, she would slip away from him. Suddenly her hand squeezed his lightly, and he looked up, her brown eyes half-mast and staring down at him.

"Brooks, what happened?" she croaked out in question, her eyes meeting his.

"You're in the hospital. You passed out, and I found you," he informed her, meeting her gaze. "You had a high fever and were severely dehydrated."

Georgie's eyes darted around the room, glancing over to the heart monitor and IV line in her hand, and her tired eyes filled with tears.

"I'm so sorry." She cried, her voice coming out hoarse and raspy.

"No, Beautiful, no," he said, rising from the chair at her bedside and cupping her face with his hands. "You're here, you're okay, and that's all that matters."

Bea peeked into the room, her smile warm and eyes compassionate. "I thought I heard voices." She said, coming into the room, striding over to them and resting her hand on Georgie's shoulder. "I'm going to take your vitals and get the doctor in here to see you, okay?"

Georgie nodded as Brooks stepped away, watching as Bea did her physical assessment and excused herself from the room.

"The wedding." Georgie breathed out, meeting his watery gaze.

"I think we need to consider postponing it. I know you want to get married right away, and you know I do too, but you need to get better first. You have five chemo treatments left, and they are only going to get more intense. I want you to enjoy our wedding and not worry about getting sick on your wedding day," he said, smoothing his hand over hers and giving it a squeeze.

"Hello, Ms. Donahue?" a tall young male doctor greeted as he entered the room and gave Brooks an acknowledging glance. "I'm Dr. Bristol, and I was the doctor on call when you came into the emergency." Flipping through her chart, he continued, "I see here that you are in the middle of chemotherapy for HER-3 breast cancer, is that correct?"

"Yes," she replied.

"Side effects of chemotherapy can sometimes be disabling. It's not uncommon for you to get a fever up to a week after a course of drugs. I'm concerned, however, about your not getting enough fluid. It's important to drink plenty of water and try to eat, although I know chemo can alter your ability to taste what you consume. If you don't hydrate properly, chemo side effects won't be your only problem. Dehydration can cause long-term damage to organs, so giving your body what it needs is important, especially right now as you undergo treatment."

"I understand." She nodded, knitting her brows together. "I have also been getting numbness in my fingers, and my hands hurt terribly. It's been hard to hold things because I can't always feel them."

"That's called Neuropathy, and it's pretty common in chemotherapy patients. You will probably experience it in your legs and feet as well. It's hard to adjust to, so you may consider a wheelchair when it flares up and/or need help to get around." The doctor informed as his gaze zoned in on Brooks. "Is this your husband, boyfriend?" he asked.

"Fiancé," she smiled. "This is Brooks."

He turned to Brooks and gave him a polite nod, addressing him directly; he continued. "Georgie is going to need extra care in the week after her treatments and likely will need someone to check in on her frequently between each treatment. They will surely get a lot more intense from here out, so are you or is there anyone you know that could provide that care? I can recommend some home care services if you need them . We just want to ensure her drinking and eating is being monitored so we aren't making another trip to the emergency."

"Yeah, I think I can make arrangements." Brooks replied, giving Georgie a reassuring look.

"Good. Okay well, I would like to keep you here one more night, get some more fluids into you, and then you should be good to go home sometime later tomorrow." He said, meeting her gaze. "Chemo is no joke, but it does save lives. You hang in there, Ms. Donahue."

With that, the doctor left, leaving them alone again. Brooks took a seat on the edge of her bed and said, "I'm going to see if I can get a leave of absence from work so I can be with you all the time," he said. "It's not safe for you to be home alone."

"Brooks, no. As much as I would love to have you around all the time, I'm sure my mom can help, and we can ask friends too, and if they can't, there is always the home care thing that the doctor mentioned." She said. "You need to work; you have bills to pay. We'll gather a team and make something work."

Brooks leaned forward, his forehead connecting with hers and his eyes lifting to meet her gaze. He swallowed hard, all the worry and emotion of the past two months rising to the surface and threatening to overflow. "I just can't see you like that again," he managed as tears pricked his eyes. "I've never been so scared in my entire life."

* * *

WITH THE WEDDING POSTPONED INDEFINITELY, Brooks and Georgie settled into a new routine. As her treatments continued, a rotation of friends and family took turns during the day. Most times their duties were light, more just hanging out, talking, watching movies or TV, making sure she ate, drank, and rested. Some days were intense when the sickness from the treatment overtook her. At night when Brooks was home from work, those were her favorite times. Times she cherished. If it weren't for the daily laughter and jokes and those quiet times when he simply held her, she was sure she would have fallen into the deep chasm of depression.

On one of those nights, Brooks was simply running his fingers through her hair as she rested her head on his lap while they watched TV. He massaged her scalp; the feel of his touch was blissfully soothing. Suddenly he stilled, and Georgie glanced up to see Brooks holding a chunk of her hair in his fingers.

"Georgie, I..." he said apologetically, his eyes transfixed on the long strands between his fingers.

Georgie rose from the couch, looked at the hair in his hand and shook her head in resolution. "It was only a matter of time." She said with a sigh. "C'mon, Big Guy. Let's go play barbershop."

30 minutes later, Georgie was sporting an incredibly shiny bald head, and Brooks was admiring his barbering skills in the mirror.

"It may just be me, but I think you have the most beautiful head I've ever seen," he said, rubbing his hands over the smooth surface of her scalp.

"Thanks." Georgie laughed, reaching up and feeling it for herself, then checking out her profile on each side. "Not bad, Big Guy."

His eyes brightened and turned playful as they met hers in the mirror. "What did the barber say to the bald person when they entered the salon?"

Georgie rolled her eyes and answered, "I don't know what?"

"What are you doing hair?"

"Oh my God, Brooks, how long have you been saving that one up for?" She asked, turning to face him, and hooking her arms around his neck.

"A while," he replied with a smirk, his face turning serious. "But all cheesy jokes aside. You are beautiful,

Georgie, and making you laugh is the highlight of my day."

* * *

BROOKS WAS EXHAUSTED, and he hadn't slept properly in months. Every time he closed his eyes, all he saw was Georgie lying on the kitchen floor, lifeless. The fear that he had lost her in that moment was real, and he was struggling. He needed to talk to someone, and the first person he could think of was his sister, Falyn.

Driving up to Prairie Charm Bed and Breakfast, he took in the pretty grounds. The bed-and-breakfast comprised two buildings. The guesthouse with its story-book castle-like features contained six guest rooms, a great room, dining room and kitchen. The second building on the property was her personal home, a cute little European-style cottage with dark wood shutters and matching window boxes for planting flowers in the spring. Both buildings had loads of character, and he could see all the work she had put into making it appealing to her guests. With Christmas three weeks away, the house was decorated with green garlands and bright red and gold bows. The entire scene was like one of those Hallmark movies that Georgie loved, and Brooks couldn't help smiling as he took it all in. Walking up to the front door, he entered and spotted Falyn handing keys to a couple who were checking in at the front desk.

"Hey Brooks," she said, as the couple disappeared up the stairs. "What brings you to Prairie Charm?"

"I was wondering if you had time to talk," he asked, meeting her gaze.

"Anytime, you know that," she said, her brows drawing together in concern as she rounded the front desk to join him. "Let's go into the great room."

Brooks followed her into a large room with different areas set up for seating. With its dark reclaimed wood beams, high ceiling and in the room's center, a spectacular stone fireplace that spanned floor to ceiling. The room was decked out for the holidays, complete with a gigantic Douglas fir tree in one corner, decorated with beautiful handmade ornaments and ribbon for garland. Everything about the room was welcoming and oozed Christmas country charm.

"This place is amazing." Brooks said, taking it all in. "I'm so proud of you, Falyn."

"Thanks. I love this room. I was thinking if you and Georgie still want to get married here after she's done treatment, we could have the ceremony here and you two could get married in front of that fireplace. I think it would make such a pretty backdrop for photos."

Brooks smiled, but it quickly faded as the memory of why they had to postpone the wedding came back.

"What's going on, Brooks?" Falyn asked, leaning over, and reaching across the couch to touch his hand. "Is Georgie okay?"

That was a loaded question. *Was she okay? Were they okay?* Seeing her so weak, feeling so low and discouraged, was difficult. And even though he did his best to keep things upbeat with his jokes and humor, doing everything in his power to make her smile and stay positive, his façade was starting to crack.

"It's just really hard right now," he said, looking down at his hands. "Georgie is so discouraged, and I don't know how to stay positive for her when I feel like all I want to do is break myself. I'm tired, Falyn. Just so exhausted, and I feel so incredibly guilty about it because I'm not the one fighting cancer. She has been so sick with these last treatments, and the only reprieve she gets is when she sleeps. Which is fitful because she's in so much pain. It's just a vicious cycle."

Falyn squeezed his hand and slid closer to him on the couch. Pulling him into her arms, she hugged him, and he let out a long exhale, returning her embrace. Tears started to fill his eyes, and his shoulders started to shake as all the fear and emotion of the last couple of months came out in a flood onto his sister's shoulder. Falyn didn't say anything, simply held him as he cried. That was one of things he appreciated about his sister. She didn't try to fill the silence with empty words to try to console him. There really were no words that could be said. No words poignant enough to bring him peace in this situation.

"Seriously, I feel like a blubbering idiot." Brooks said with a pained chuckle as he let go of his sister and wiped at his face.

"Stop being so self-deprecating." Falyn scolded, swatting his arm lightly. "You have every right to feel these feelings. The woman you have loved for more than half your life is fighting for her life, and it's damn scary."

Brooks nodded as he confessed, "Seeing Georgie on the floor passed out, I honestly thought she was dead.

That was my first thought. Georgie had died, and I wasn't there. I don't think I've been more terrified in my entire life."

"I can't imagine, Brooks," she said, shaking her head and meeting his eyes. "I can't imagine that kind of fear. But Brooks, you can't live in that fear. Georgie is here still very much alive; that's what you need to focus on. You've done everything you can to keep her safe since that day. You need to know you have done an incredible job. Please tell me you know that."

"Georgie has told me that and her family of course, but it's hard when it's just not enough. I want to protect her from the monsters, and all I can do is watch them attack her."

* * *

CHEMOTHERAPY SUCKS. *That is all.* Every 21 days proved to be the test of Georgie's strength. Going through month after month of treatments with endless cycles of fevers, chills, night sweats, vomiting and gastrointestinal issues had become her norm, and waking up every morning felt like Groundhog Day as she did it all over again. As her side effects worsened, so did her mental health. She spent days thinking about what she was missing, worrying about how Brooks and her family were coping and hyper-focusing on her uncertain future. Being that she was a therapist, she understood the human psyche, and yet she couldn't get herself out of the funk.

"Georgie, are you up for a visitor?" her mother asked as she came into the living room from the kitchen.

Georgie lifted her head from her pillow, and sat up, everything hurting as she straightened out her Kicking Cancer's Ass togue covering her bald head and pulled her blanket up over her shoulders. "Sure," she replied, her own voice sounding hollow and weak, as the famous Ms. Mable entered the room.

Ms. Mable was a retired school bus driver and a legend in the community of Primrose. As the sister of town librarian, Ms. Lynette, she was involved in every committee, at the forefront of town beautification, and was loved and respected by young and old alike. Now in her late 70s, she was white-haired, spry, and still as feisty as ever.

"Why, hello there, Georgie, Porgie, pudding and pie," she said as she entered the room carrying a small terra-cotta pot with a cute little round cactus.

Georgie couldn't help but smile. Ms. Mable was the only one who still dared to call her that after all these years. "Hi, Ms. Mable. This is a nice surprise."

"I was just in the neighbourhood, and I heard you were feeling a little down these days." She said with a frown as she set her hand on her Georgie's knee. Her frown turned quickly to a hesitant smile as she added, "I thought I would come visit and hopefully cheer you up a bit." Ms. Mable set down the little cactus on the coffee table and turned to face her, narrowing her eyes as she took her in. "I would like to say you look fantastic, but let's call a spade a spade. You look dreadful, my dear."

Georgie sputtered out a laugh. That was the Ms. Mable everyone knew and loved. Blunt and always speaks her mind. Georgie shrugged as she responded. "Yeah, I'm kind of in a battle these days, and I'm getting tired of fighting."

Ms. Mable gave her an empathetic smile and nodded. "I remember how that was, Georgie."

Georgie blinked in surprise, her words hitting her square in the chest as she asked, "You had cancer?"

"Yep, breast cancer stage three, the same as you." She answered matter-of - factly. "I was 28 when I was diagnosed."

"Younger than me." Georgie replied, still trying to process this new piece of information.

"Yes, I was young, newly married, and we were trying to have a family at the time." She said. I was so tired and honestly had convinced myself that I was pregnant, but when all the blood tests came back, it turned out I had cancer."

"That's a kick in the teeth." Georgie replied. "I would've been devastated."

"I was. I honestly felt like all my hopes and dreams were taken away from me with that one word. If it weren't for my Leo, I think I probably would've given up," she said with a nostalgic smile. "My husband, Leo, kept my mind positive, and he always made me laugh. He kind of reminds me of your Brooks, actually."

"I think I would have given up by now if it weren't for Brooks," Georgie confessed. "He's been with me at every treatment and has never wavered. I know he's scared and exhausted, but he does whatever he can to try to keep me smiling. I'm so grateful for that, and I love him so much."

"Brooks loves you; I could see that even when you were kids. That boy has been smitten with you darn near all his life." She said with a little laugh that was reflective and sweet as she picked up the little cactus she brought with her.

"Now, you're probably wondering why I brought you this little guy, aren't you?" she asked, carefully holding it between her two hands.

Georgie smiled, looking down at the cute little plant, and nodded.

"This little fella is one of the most resilient plants in the world. It symbolizes strength, endurance, and protection. It can survive in harsh environments and protects itself with its tough exterior. You, Georgie, are this little cactus, and every time you look at it and feel like it's all too much, I want you to remember that you are tough and resilient, just like this little plant." She said, setting the plant down on the coffee table in front of her.

Georgie swallowed down a lump that had formed in her throat as tears welled up in her eyes. Glancing towards the little plant, her eyes drifted over to meet Ms. Mable's supportive gaze. "Thank you. I needed to hear this," Georgie rasped out, as she wiped at a tear that escaped down her cheek.

"I thought you might." Ms. Mable said, her smile wide as she patted Georgie's knee and rose from the couch. "Well, I best be going. Hit me up on Facebook if you have any questions or need another kick in the pants."

Georgie giggled through her tears and looked down again at her little cactus, feeling like she could and would get through this for the first time in months.

CHAPTER 11

Knowing the end of chemotherapy was near, Georgie's spirits were high. The past months had been the most challenging of her life. Trying to stay positive despite her painful symptoms was next to impossible, but she had done it. She had done it with Brooks by her side. He had been unwavering, a pillar of strength when she couldn't find hers, and through that her love for him grew stronger.

Brooks pulled into the treatment centre parking lot for the last time and turned to meet Georgie's gaze. She smiled wearily at him as she rested her head back against the seat.

"This is it," he said, reaching up and caressing her cheek tenderly. "Last chemo."

"Last chemo." She echoed as she cocked an eyebrow at him. "Let's give this disease one last kick in the ass."

"That's my girl," he said with a smile. "Did you know I've heard like seven cancer jokes today?" Georgie giggled and rolled her eyes as he delivered the punchline. "If I hear tumour, it will benign."

Georgie shook her head with a chuckle and hooked her finger, beckoning Brooks towards her. He obliged, drawing closer; his lips hovering over hers. Georgie cupped his face, looking deep into his eyes. "I love you, Brooks Isley. Thank you for loving me through this."

With that, Brooks bridged the gap. All the worry, all the pain and all the fear of the past months suddenly evaporated with one reverent kiss.

IT HAD BEEN two months since her last chemo treatment, and for the first time in a long time, Georgie felt strong enough to do a therapy session. She knew she wouldn't be riding anytime soon, but working with the horses and clients gave her a purpose again. And all she wanted was to feel some normalcy. Finishing up the session, she heard a vehicle pull up to the barn and a door slam. Closing the box stall she turned to see Brooks leaning against the cased opening of the barn, his long, large body clad in his dusty work overalls work boots casually crossed at the ankles and for the first time in a long time, she felt completely turned on by the sight of him. They hadn't had sex in months, her desires squashed by the brutal drugs pumping through her body. It wasn't uncommon for sexual desire to wane during treatment. Georgie had read all the brochures. Yet, it was during those exhausting days, her body weak, that her mind wandered to the very beginning when she couldn't get enough of him, and he was ready and willing to satisfy any and all of her desires.

"You're looking at me like you want to eat me," he said, sauntering over and giving her a coy smile as he settled his hands on her hips. "Penny for your thoughts, Beautiful?"

"Just checking out my fiancé." She replied, going on her tiptoes to hook her arms around his neck.

"Are you admiring my ruggedly handsome looks or my luscious dad bod?" he asked smoothly, lifting her into his arms, his large palms squeezing her behind.

"Both," she replied, as she leaned in and kissed him tentatively at first, but when he squeezed her ass again, and she felt the unmistakable evidence of his desire, she moaned into his mouth, deepening their embrace. They kissed passionately, their tongues finding a rhythm that was sensual and needy. Brooks carried her over to a stack of hay bales, placed her on top and reluctantly pulled his lips away.

"What do you need, Beautiful?" he asked, his breaths coming out heavy and wanton.

"I need you to touch me," she replied. "It's been too long, and I want everything with you, but right now, I just need to be touched."

Brooks smiled, his eyes darkening as he breached the waist of her riding pants, his large hand making its way lower to cup her sex. His calloused fingers dipped between her folds to be met with her warm wet desire.

"Georgie," he growled, as he slid a digit up and down her slit, circling her pulse point of pleasure.

She threw her head back, the feeling of being touched

after so long both surreal and painfully exquisite. His fingers worked her methodically, just the way she liked, until she was panting and begging for release.

"Please, Brooks, I need more." She cried out. "Make me come."

Brooks smiled, his grin wicked and so provocative as his large body loomed over her. With her request, he dipped a finger into her molten heat, finding the tender spot in her inner wall, and caressed it as he circled her centre with his thumb. The pleasure of her release surged through her body, and she couldn't hold herself up. Suddenly feeling weak. Brooks, sensing this, cradled her body as she shook with her orgasm sparking through her.

With languid caresses until she came down, Brooks removed his hand and scooped her up, holding her protectively in his arms. She sighed, kissing his jaw, his cheek, his mouth. "Thank you. I want to do more, but I..."

"Georgie, I know you do. It's going to take some time." Brooks reassured her , kissing her softly as he held her. "Whenever you're ready, I'll be ready. However long it takes. I do, however, have something to ask you though."

"Anything." she replied, staring up at him with curiosity.

"Will you go out on a date with me?" he asked, meeting her curious gaze.

Georgie giggled and nuzzled into his neck. "I guess we've never actually gone out on a date, have we?"

"Nope. We went from friends to lovers to living together to engaged in the blink of an eye," he replied. "I think we have some backtracking to do."

* * *

FRIDAY NIGHT, date night and Georgie was beside herself with excitement. Having gotten plenty of rest during the day, she felt surprisingly energetic and ready for whatever Brooks had planned. Glancing at herself in the mirror, she saw that her once long hair had now grown back into a flattering short pixie style. She stared at herself in the mirror, taking in her features, now more angled and sharper with the weight loss. Having her port still in place due to monthly injections required to help block the growth of any other cancer cells, she chose a knee length form fitted red sweater dress that covered her port and hugged whatever curves she had left. Georgie hated how the disease had changed her body, but right now as she stared at her reflection, she made the conscious decision to embrace her body the way it was now, knowing her mastectomy surgery was on the horizon. She still wasn't sure how she felt about it. If she could save her breasts, she would, but with her type of cancer, surgery was the most preventative way for her to ensure she would never have to go through breast cancer again. The thought, however, made her anxious and, if she was being honest with herself, downright scared. Not so much about the surgery itself but about the impact it would have on her physical relationship with Brooks. *Will he see me as attractive? Will he be disgusted by my scars? Will he think of me as half a woman?* Although deep down in her heart she knew that the answer to all these questions was no, it still worried her.

Tamping down her feelings about the subject, she

reached for her purse and headed downstairs to where Brooks was waiting for her. Coming into the kitchen, she glanced around. No Brooks. Popping her head into the living room and not seeing him there, she peeked outside at the backyard and patio. Frowning and a little confused as to where Brooks had gone, his crazy doorbell sounded, and Georgie made her way to the door to answer it. Swinging the door open, Brooks stood there, dressed handsomely in a navy button-down shirt, blazer, tan chinos and shined up leather shoes. In his hand was a large bouquet of colorful roses, vibrant yellow, orange, red, pink, and white. It was the most beautiful bouquet that Georgie had ever seen.

"You must be Georgie Donahue," he said, feigning nervousness as he handed her the bouquet.

Georgie met his eyes, playfulness in their depths as she accepted the bouquet. "These are amazing, thank you," she said as she held them up to her nose, deeply inhaling their sweet floral scent. Glancing up at him through her lashes, he gave her an impish grin as he lingered on the front step awkwardly. Realizing that he wasn't going to take a step in until she invited him to, she said with a giggle, "Please come in, Brooks, is it?"

Brooks nodded, looked down at her, mischief in his eyes as he replied, "I don't usually go on blind dates, but I have to say, their description did not do you justice. You are breathtaking, Ms. Donahue."

This is a fun little game.

"Thank you, Brooks, and you're very handsome." She complimented, her voice dripping with flirtation as she boldly let her eyes roam up and down his body. "I wasn't sure what to expect, and well, you did not disappoint."

Brooks cocked an eyebrow at her, drawing a little closer, his eyes darkening a shade, and as the look she knew so well sparkled in his eyes. He wanted to kiss her, but right now they were role-playing and this was a first date. Placing her hand on his chest, she said, "Let me quickly put these into a vase." Brooks nodded, following her into the kitchen as she prepared a vase and set the flowers in it, placing it on the kitchen table. Turning to face Brooks, his eyes combed her body, flashing with approval as they returned to the front entrance, and she reached for her coat. "Please allow me," he said, taking the coat from her grasp. Turning around, he helped her into the sleeves, and as he slipped it onto her shoulders, he leaned in, his hot breath caressing her ear. The move was so slight, but it caused her to suck in a breath as her body awakened and goosebumps rose on her skin.

Reaching for her purse, she turned and hooked her arm through his as he led her out of the house to his truck. Opening the door for her, she grinned, the whole chivalrous gentleman routine a nice touch. Brooks rounded the truck and climbed inside, turning to face her.

"How does Mexican food sound?"

Heavenly. Having lost most of her appetite and taste during treatments, the thought of rich or decadent food now was almost an aphrodisiac. She locked eyes with Brooks, a sexy smile curling her lips as she replied, "Why, Mr. Isley, it's as if you know me. If this weren't a first date, I would think you were trying to seduce me."

* * *

PULLING into one of their favorite restaurants, the Blue Corn, Brooks continued his chivalry, opening doors and offering his arm as they entered the restaurant and were seated in a quiet booth in the corner. Sliding in next to her, they placed their orders, two virgin margaritas and a combination plate with a little of all their favorite dishes as they settled into the booth.

Taking a sip of his lime margarita, Brooks surveyed Georgie as if seeing her for the first time. To an outsider, she looked like a gorgeous, healthy woman, but knowing the hell her body and mind had been through over the past months, he couldn't help but look at her differently. Having known Georgie most of his life, there was no question she was a strong, feisty, and determined woman, but now as he stared into her gorgeous brown eyes, his love and respect for her seemed to have multiplied tenfold. He loved her before, but now, seeing her here, so bright and alive, his adoration, respect, and boundless love for her were staggering.

Georgie leaned in, resting her hand on his thigh, and his breath hitched as she gave it a flirtatious squeeze and looked at him, her eyes dancing with mirth. "I know we don't know each other that well yet, Mr. Isley, but I think after tonight we'll know each other so much better."

Brooks felt his arousal perk up at her tawdry prediction. Throughout her treatment and over the past couple of months as she continued with post-chemo injections, he hadn't pushed the bounds of physicality with her. Seeing her in so much pain, her treatments having ravaged her in ways he couldn't fully understand, his needs had to be shelved, and he was more than okay with doing so. Despite his imposed celibacy, his desire for Georgie never waned, just grew deeper, simmering inside of him until it was ready to overflow. Tonight could be that night, when he could have all of her again, but she would have to be the one to give him the green light. For now, though, they would play this cute little game they had started.

"Why, Ms. Donahue, you're so forward. Maybe I'm not that kind of man." he replied cheekily, clutching his chest.

Georgie laughed, the sound so melodic and beautiful it made emotions rise to the surface. *Oh, how I love her laugh.*

Their food arrived, breaking him from his revelry, and Georgie's eyes lit up. The heavenly scent of slow-cooked meat, spicy chilis, acidic lime, warm tortillas, rich beans, and savory rice permeated the air around them, and Georgie leaned in breathing deeply the delicious smell. Her eyes rolled back, and Brooks smiled in amusement as he loaded his fork with a little of everything from the plate and brought it to her mouth. Georgie's eyes shone with delight as she took the offered bite and fell back against the booth, her hand covering her mouth as she chewed. Mumbling through her bite, she declared, "Oh, my God, that is the best bite of my life."

Brooks laughed as he filled his fork again, feeding Georgie, and her willingly accepting every morsel. Watching her enjoy food again was a joy he had no words for. So, he continued to feed her until Georgie leaned back against her seat, resting her hand on her stomach.

"I can't eat another bite," she stated with a resolute

sigh. "I'm still trying to get my appetite back, so you enjoy the rest."

Brooks caressed her cheek lovingly as she rested her head on his shoulder while he ate, reveling in the simple pleasure of this time with his girl.

* * *

AFTER DINNER, they drove out of St. Augustine heading towards Primrose just as the sun was making its final descent into the horizon. Darkness blanketing the bare fields, Georgie stared out the passenger window as stars started to dapple the night sky. Turning to face Brooks, she asked, "Do you think we could go to our secret place?"

"Sure," he replied, reaching for her hand and giving it a squeeze. "It'll be dark, but we could stargaze from the top of the culvert."

"Yes, I'd like that."

Driving just past Primrose, Brooks turned onto the gravel road, their intersection quickly approaching as he slowed down, parking just before the juncture of the two roads. Getting out of the cab, Brooks came around the front of the vehicle, opened Georgie's door and helped her climb out of the truck.

"I'm going to go first and help you down the embankment, okay?" he said, the darkness enveloping them both. "It hasn't rained in a while, but I don't know if the rocks will be slippery."

She nodded as he went ahead of her, halfway down, turning to take her hand as they carefully climbed down the embankment until they reached the corrugated metal top of the culvert. Taking a seat first, Brooks helped Georgie down to sit next to him. Their feet dangled off the edge. Brooks wrapped his arm around her and pulled her in closer. They both looked up, as a million stars twinkling overhead.

"I always wanted to do this," Georgie said in a whisper. "Come out here at night. See the stars. It's beautiful."

"It is." Brooks replied. "It was a good idea."

They sat there a long time, wrapped around each other, the spring night breeze cool as it rustled the long grass of the ditch.

"This is the most peace I've felt in a long time. The past months have been so full of uncertainties, and well, right here, right now, it feels like anything is possible." Georgie said wistfully. "Like, it was when we were kids."

"Carefree," Brooks added.

"Carefree," Georgie echoed, as she turned to face Brooks. His silhouette was shrouded by darkness but visible in the moonlight, she asked, "How did you do it? Get through the past months."

"It wasn't easy." Brooks confessed. "There were so many days when you were so sick, not able to walk or get out of bed, and I would just sit and watch you sleep. The whole time praying that you still had strength to get through it. It's hard seeing the person you love more than life itself suffering and knowing there is nothing you can do to take the pain away."

"I'm sorry you had to go through that." Georgie said, resting her head on his shoulder.

"I wouldn't want to be anywhere else, Beautiful. I will

always be by your side, no matter what life throws at us," he said, planting a kiss on her head.

"You know, there's something else we never did in this secret place of ours," she said, her voice dripping with flirtation.

"What's that?"

"Kiss."

"Well then, we must change that immediately," he said, lifting her onto his lap, holding onto her securely so she wouldn't fall. Cupping her cheek, she could make out the twinkle in his eye and the outline of his lips. "You know, my 16-year-old self is cheering right now. You realize that, don't you?"

"Did you fantasize about kissing me when we were teenagers?" She asked with a giggle.

"Every damn day!" he exclaimed. "Sometimes you were even who I visualized when I..."

"Brooks, no!" she gasped. "You did not!"

"I can neither confirm nor deny. Let's just say those were some confusing years," he replied with a chuckle. "Okay, fantasy girl, where are those lips?" he asked, feeling her face in the darkness and making her giggle more. As the tips of fingers grazed over her bottom lip, he leaned in, capturing her mouth in a hungry kiss. Georgie matched him, her desire awakening low in her belly as his tongue teased her lips to open. Her lips parted, their tongues tangling in the way they did so well. One arm cradling her, they kissed like two horny teenagers with only the stars there to witness.

* * *

WITH A MIND-BLOWING make-out session stoking the flames, the energy between them was palpable. They hadn't been with each other in months, Brooks, a pinnacle of restraint and patience through it all. Tonight, however, the drought would end. Georgie was going to make love to Brooks, her fiancé, and the only man she ever loved. Locking the door behind them, the charged heat radiating off Brooks was fervent as he bridged the gap between them and devoured her lips, his large palm sliding to the back of her head to brace her. They kissed as if they were thirsty and only this passionate kiss could quench their insatiable thirst. It was raw, needy, wanton. A kiss that staked claim and put the uncertainty of the past months firmly in the rearview mirror. It was now just the two of them, so in love it was both painful and perfect, in the same breath.

Pulling his lips away, chest heaving in a breath, Brooks scooped Georgie into his arms and carried her up the stairs to their bedroom. Setting her down beside the bed, he reached for the hem of her dress and lifted it slowly, his eyes trained on hers as he undressed her. His hungry eyes roamed over her, and she could see in his gaze that he noticed the toll her cancer had taken on her body. Where there was once supple fullness, and ample curves, there was a thin frailty in its place. Their eyes met, and Georgie gave him a look of apprehension as she spoke.

"I know I'm not the same woman I once was," she managed with a shaky voice, as she blinked back the unexpected tears that were brimming. "But I hope you'll love me, anyway."

"Georgie, Beautiful, I love you more," he declared,

cupping her face in his hands, and wiping away her traitorous tears with his thumbs. "Your body has changed; you and I both know that. I wish you didn't have to go through what you went through, but your body has proven itself to be resilient and strong, and no matter your shape or size, I find you incredibly sexy."

"Even after the mastectomy?" She asked, looking down at her chest. "Because I know how much you like the girls." Brooks laughed and shook his head at her comment, making Georgie let out a nervous giggle of her own, the seriousness of their conversation replaced with their trademark silliness. "Brooks, stop, I'm serious." She chided, giving him a playful swat on the arm. "There won't be anything left for you to fondle. Seriously, Brooks, they will be gone."

"Nothing left for me to fondle." he repeated, gripping her behind and pulling her closer, his large palms kneading the flesh. "I happen to be extra fond of your ass if you haven't noticed."

She smiled, moaning as he pressed his rather impressive ridge into her, and her eyes met his dark and hungry. "I will love and worship every part of you that is left and know when I say that I mean it. You, Georgie, are so much more than the sum of your parts. Please tell me you know that."

"I know, it's just I..." she started, but before she could counter, he crushed his lips to hers. She melted into him; her body pliant under his touch as their kiss turned from a spark to a wildfire. They kissed, seeking, nothing deep enough to ease the ache and need to be with each other again. Pulling away, her lips swollen, and kiss bitten she said, "Don't be gentle with me tonight. I'll tell you if it's all too much, but I don't want you to hold back and think you're going to break me. I'm not fragile, and I want to be thoroughly fucked; do you understand me?"

Brooks' pupils dilated so dark the blue simply rimmed the edges as he questioned, "Is that what you need?"

"Yes," she breathed out.

With that he spun her, making her gasp, her back to his chest as he leaned in, his breath hot against the shell of her ear. "Get naked and kneel on the bed," he growled, making goosebumps form on her skin. She did as she was told, discarding her bra and panties as she climbed onto the bed, the anticipation of what came next causing her core to clench with need. She could hear him undress, and the end table drawer open, the familiar crinkle of the foil packet making her breaths come out shuddered with awareness. With his weight dipping the bed and his hands on her hips, he slipped his fingers between her folds, her sensitive flesh swollen with her desire. Brooks growled, the sound almost animalistic as he found her wet and ready for him. The sound of the foil pack being ripped open came next, and then he was there, the large crown of him pressing into her, her head falling forward as the exquisite pressure of Brooks filling her overtook her senses. It was sweet torture, and she had forgotten how much she craved this feeling of being filled and consumed. How much she craved him.

"Oh God, Brooks!" she cried out as inch by glorious inch he filled the space inside her that longed for this primal connection.

"Are you okay, Beautiful?" he asked, leaning over her, the air around them charged with desire.

"Yes, it's so good," she breathed out as she clutched the comforter. "I've missed the way you feel inside me."

"And I've missed you too," he replied on an exhale pumping in and out of her, each slide hitting a spot inside her that was sure to make her lose control. Moaning with each thrust, his hands guided her hips to meet each one, the slap of their skin and his growls of carnal pleasure taking her higher.

"Go faster, Brooks," she begged, feeling the orgasm she was chasing start to crest.

Quickening his pace, he pounded into her, reaching an impossibly deep place with each punishing thrust until her body gave in to the blinding pleasure only he could give her. Sparks, stars, fireworks went off inside her body, each nerve ending igniting with sensation as her orgasm ripped through her.

"That's it, Beautiful," he groaned, unbridled desire dripping from his words. "I've missed this, the feel of you gripping me."

Unrelenting, he rode out her wave of pleasure as he found his own, his body stilling behind her as he let out a low, rumbly growl that was raw and sensual. The feel of him swelling and pulsing inside her, unbelievably erotic. With a few more shuddering thrusts, he pulled her up and pressed her back to his chest, his arms around her waist.

"That was incredible," he breathed out as he planted a trail of kisses down the column of her neck and wrapped his strong arms around her body. "I've missed us."

CHAPTER 12

Georgie woke the next morning, deliciously sore and feeling blissfully satisfied. They had reacquainted themselves with each other's bodies thoroughly last night and, for the first time in a long time, she felt somewhat normal.

Brooks stirred at her back as he pulled her into him, his hand resting on her stomach. She loved how warm he always was and how even when she was in the trenches of treatment, experiencing the chills that often came with the side effects, he had the ability to warm her up. Lacing her fingers through his, she thought about the future, what she wanted with him and the impending joy that marriage and growing a family would bring. The thought of carrying their baby, her belly round and full, his large palms cradling it as he gazed upon her with so much love and adoration in his eyes. The picture in her mind's eye, sheer perfection. They would have a life after all this was done, and she would give him what he desired. The marriage, the family, all of it. The only unknown question was, would her body allow her to? Could she carry a baby after the ravages of the chemo drugs? Her period hadn't returned in the months after treatment, and according to her doctor, that was normal, but would she be able to conceive at all if her body never resumed regular function? The thought of that created a cavernous void in her heart, but she needed to be ready for that possibility. Georgie let out a long-pained exhale, and the deep timber of Brooks' voice broke the silence.

"Is everything okay, Georgie?" he asked. "You don't sigh like that unless you're troubled by something."

Damn him for knowing me so well. Georgie rolled over to face him, his eyes searching hers as she sighed again and prepared herself for this difficult conversation.

"Lay it on me, Georgie," he urged. "You're still my best friend and always will be. No matter how much our relationship has evolved."

"Yeah, I know. It's just something I need to discuss with my doctor. I'm worried about not being able to give you a family. I mean, I know women who've been through chemo can get pregnant, but my body is not functioning normally, and I worry that it never will."

Brooks' adam's apple bobbed as he swallowed, her eyes following the movement. Hearing this had to be difficult as it was like saying a lifelong dream could never come true. Brooks deserved to be a father, and she couldn't live with herself if she took that away from him. *But is it me taking it from him, or the disease?* Feeling overwhelmed, her head full of unanswered questions, she buried her face in his chest. Brooks smoothed his hand through her short hair, his fingertips caressing her scalp, soothing her. He let out a long, stuttering breath and replied, "Georgie, we'll figure it out. If we can't have a child of our own, we'll adopt a child that needs us. Either way, we will be parents someday I promise you that."

Georgie took in his promise for what she was sure it was. A consolation prize in the life he had envisioned for them.

* * *

ENTERING THE EAZY CAFÉ, Brooks spotted Kolt, Hayden Hastings and his cousin Jaxon Isley occupying a booth at the back of the diner. Kolt waved him over, and he made his way between the tables, fielding smiles and greetings from the local farmers that he frequently conversed with at the feed mill.

"Hey," he said, sliding into the booth next to Kolt. "I feel like I haven't seen all of you in a lifetime."

"It's been a while." Jaxon echoed. "How are you and Georgie doing? My mom mentioned she saw her the other day and said she looked good. Happy and healthier."

Brooks smiled as he replied, "She's slowly getting back to normal. Still has a few more months of injections before she's done with that phase. Also, surgery is on the horizon, which I know she's very anxious about. That part will be hard."

"What did she decide regarding surgery?" Kolt asked with concern in his tone.

"Full mastectomy." Brooks replied as the table quieted, their respect for the situation evident. "Honestly, the only thing I care about is that she's cancer free and stays that way. I know she's nervous that it will change how I view her, and lately she's been completely obsessed with the future. What we will have, what we may not have. Truly nothing else matters to me but having her by my side."

"You're a good man," Hayden said, giving him a little nudge under the table. "If Whitney was in Georgie's shoes, I would feel the same way. All that would matter is her health in the long term."

"What about the future is worrying her?" Kolt asked, furrowing his brows.

"Her ability to have children." Brooks replied matter-of-factly.

"That's a sensitive subject." Jaxon replied. "It's a completely different situation, but when Dee and I went through our fertility challenges, it was emotional. There was so much uncertainty going on, even though our situation ended up being easier than we thought. I can't imagine what Georgie is going through right now."

Brooks leaned against the vinyl backrest and let out a long exhale. "There's a real possibility that the chemo drugs have rendered her unable to have children. She's going to talk to her doctor, see if we can get a referral to a fertility specialist and see what kinds of options we have. My fear is that once we have answers, and if those answers aren't in our favor, she's going to see herself as failing me. But honestly, whether we have biological children together or not, it doesn't matter to me. We have so many options for becoming parents. And if none of those work out, I will still be happy because all I want and need is her. I've told her as much, but it's like she doesn't believe me. It's like she thinks this is something that's going to make me change how I feel about her. Something that will make me change my mind about marrying her.

The men at the table nodded their heads, quiet contemplation falling on the group until Hayden suggested, "Maybe you need a grand gesture. When Ben and Ever were first together, she was here in Primrose just for the summer until she figured out what to do with Prairie Sky. After the summer ended, she had to return to Toronto, and they were in a sort of limbo state with their relationship. Not together, but not broken up either, and Ben was completely heartbroken about it. I know he was sure he would never see her again, so he flew out there and proposed, right there in the middle of a bunch of strangers. Ben, my brother, who is so stoic and unshakable, was so distraught with the thought of losing her that he went out of his comfort zone. Perhaps you and Georgie need a little reset. Propose to her again and maybe set a date for your wedding to remind her that you are in it for the long haul. Remind her that you love her no matter what the future holds for you both."

"That's a good idea, actually. Everything was so rushed before that I didn't even get a chance to buy her a ring." Brooks replied, leaning forward, his head reeling with ideas as a slow smile curled his lips. "We missed celebrating our birthdays this year as she was just finishing up her treatments." Brooks lit up as he smirked, mischief twinkling in his eyes as he glanced between his friends and family. "I think I know the perfect way to do this, but it's going to require all of you to get a little uncomfortable."

* * *

"I THINK we need to throw a party." Brooks exclaimed that night as they sat on the couch together eating Chinese leftovers from Ling's Family Restaurant takeout boxes while they watched a home renovation show.

"A party?" She questioned, turning to face him.

"Yeah! Like a full-out belated birthday party. Balloons, a banner, tons of food, red velvet cake and all our friends. We can have it right here. Oh, and we can add a theme!" Brooks exclaimed, his eyes beaming with excitement.

Georgie let out a giggle, thoroughly enjoying his unexpected enthusiasm. "What kind of theme were you thinking?"

"How about a "Pretty in Pink" theme?" he suggested, turning to face her. "Everyone dresses in pink, even the guys, and we'll have pink decorations. Seriously, this place will look like a cotton candy, Peptol Bismol, Barbie dreamland by the time we're done. What do you think?"

"Brooks, you're crazy!" she replied, as she set down the takeout box and rose from the couch, climbing onto his lap and planting a sweet kiss on his lips before she added, "But I love it."

* * *

AS PROMISED, BROOKS' house looked like Barbie's dream house. Pink decorations covered every surface, the table was filled with food, all of Georgie's favorites that had been dropped off ahead of time by all their friends and family, and in the middle of the table stood, a decadent two-tiered red velvet cake that Marnie had outdone herself making. The scene had been set, and the stunning solitaire diamond ring he had purchased earlier in the week was well hidden where he was certain she wouldn't find it.

Georgie's footsteps sounded on the stairs, and he turned to see her round the staircase, dressed in a sleeveless blush-colored tulle dress, with retro 1950s flair. Her short hair was styled nicely, makeup on point, showing off her gorgeous eyes and lips as well as that dimple that made his heart patter just a little faster every time she smiled. His eyes drifted over her from head to toe as he gave her a resounding look of approval and let out a little whistle.

"Pretty in Pink," he said cheekily as he took her hand and made her spin, causing the skirt of her dress to twirl. She beamed at him, hooking her arms around his neck, and beckoning him in for a kiss with her chocolate brown eyes. Lowering his head, he brushed his lips to hers, pulling her in to deepen their embrace. By the time he pulled back, Georgie was breathless, and her cheeks flushed the color of her dress. Wrapping her arms around Brooks' waist, Chewbacca sounded, making them both laugh and breaking them from the intimate moment. "It's time to party!" Brooks exclaimed, twirling her once more before he strode to the door.

Two hours later, the party was in full swing. Everyone who was near and dear to them was there, a sea of every shade of pink you could conjure up. Most of the guests had spilled into the backyard and onto the deck, where Brooks had strung up fairy lights, which were turned on as the light of day was fading.

Brooks glanced outside, seeing Georgie sitting in the corner of the yard, visiting with Falyn, Jaxon's wife Dee, and Bea Smithfield along with her husband Garrett, the chemistry teacher at Primrose High School. Brooks turned around to face his conspirators, Kolt, Hayden and Jaxon, along with several other family and friends all sporting their own versions of the "Pretty in Pink" dress.

"Are you guys ready?" Brooks asked, his eyes sparking with delight.

"Fuck Brooks, only you could get all of us into a dress." Hayden commented, looking down at his strapless, sequined cocktail number and letting out a deep laugh. "Anything to make Georgie smile, though."

"She's going to love it." Brooks replied, straightening out his enormous bra stuffed with two cantaloupes and smoothing down his bright fuchsia halter-neck ball gown.

Cueing the music that wafted into the backyard with portable speakers, Brooks' signature song, "I'm too sexy," started, and Brooks burst through the patio door, in full proud pink regalia.

* * *

GEORGIE'S EYES GREW WIDE, and a smile curled her lips as Brooks stepped out onto the deck in the largest, most gaudy pink ball gown she had ever seen.

"Oh, my God." Falyn gasped beside her as her hand

came up to her mouth, stifling a laugh that couldn't help but burst forth.

Laughter, cheers, whistles, and catcalls surrounded her from their guests, and all she managed to do was stare, flabbergasted, at the pink monstrosity that was strutting towards her. Brooks spun and posed doing his catwalk moves, shaking his tush, and whatever was stuffed in his bra almost fell out when he shimmied closer to her. *Are those cantaloupes?*

Georgie let out a giggle, cocking an eyebrow at him coyly. He waggled his eyebrows and blew her a kiss as six other men made their way down the makeshift runway, one by one draped in various pink concoctions, posing, and playing off the energy of the guests and catcalls from their wives and girlfriends. Each was more fantastic than the next, and by the time the fashion show was over, Georgie's face and sides hurt from the onslaught of laughter.

"That might be the best thing I've ever seen." Georgie giggled, turning to Falyn, Dee, Garett, and Bea, who agreed with tears of laughter in their eyes.

Their attention turned and Georgie's eyes followed them as all the guests began to sing, "Happy Birthday" in a rising chorus, Brooks still in all his pink glory, carefully carried out the birthday cake, a sea of brightly lit candles glowing in the dim light of the backyard.

Georgie stood from her lawn chair, her heart feeling so full as her eyes drifted from friend to friend, family member to family member, all singing and beaming at her with love. Brooks' mirthful eyes met hers, dancing with the flickers of the candles.

"Make a wish, Beautiful," he said.

Georgie smiled, closing her eyes to make her silent wish, then opening them slowly, locked gazes with Brooks and blew out all 31 candles. Cheers and clapping followed as Brooks handed off the cake to Hayden and Georgie combed the faces of the guests, thanking them. When Georgie turned around, her breath caught and her hand came up to her heart as she took in Brooks, down on one knee in front of her.

Brooks' sparkling blue eyes shone up at her as he met her gaze. "Georgie Donahue, I have been in love with you for as long as I can remember. You are my best friend, my lover, my hero. Your beauty, your strength and your courage have brought me to my knees here in front of you. I love you, and although technically we have done this already, I want you to know that no matter what the future has in store for us, I want you by my side for the rest of our lives. Will you marry me, Beautiful?" Brooks asked, producing a ring box out of his huge brazier, and all the guests laughed through their tears as he opened the box, revealing the gorgeous diamond ring inside. Georgie's breath caught as he took it out of the box, placed it on her ring finger and looked up at her, his eyes questioning.

"Yes!" she exclaimed as she pulled him to his feet. Trying to envelope her in a hug, his melons getting in the way, he quickly removed them, tossing them to the ground, eliciting giggles from Georgie and causing fits of laughter from their guests. Lifting her, he spun her around as he captured her lips in a joyous embrace.

Pulling back, Brooks' eyes locked on hers as he asked, "Do you like the ring?"

She held her hand out, taking in the sparkler on her finger. "It's perfect."

"You're perfect. I love you, Georgie, and I cannot wait until you are my wife."

CHAPTER 13

The day that Georgie was dreading was here. Surgery day. Brooks held her hand until the moment the operating room doors opened for her, every emotion washing over her all at once as he disappeared from her view. The pale green tiled room smelled sterile; the sound of voices echoed through the room as the anesthesiologist spoke in low tones, covered her mouth with a mask and the bright hospital lights faded to black.

Georgie heard voices, barely a whisper, the sound muffled in her hazy state of consciousness. The steady staccato beep of a heart monitor came through as the voices grew louder in her head. With Brooks, and her mother both in the room, a third voice not recognizable as she tried to open her eyes, her lids weighted down and heavy. A thin band of light appeared, growing larger as she tried to focus, the overhead hospital lights too bright. She squeezed her eyes shut, willing herself to try opening them again, until the band of light appeared once more.

"She's waking up." Her mother said, her voice now coming in crisp and clear.

Georgie squinted, her eyes fluttering open slowly as she felt Brooks' large hand encapsulate hers, the warmth of his touch comforting. Intense pain surged through her chest, and she cried out, her mother and Brooks faces contorted with worry.

"We're going to give you something for the pain, Ms. Donahue," the third voice of a nurse said. "I just need to check your vitals."

She proceeded to check her over and changed the piggyback IV bag to include medication for pain management before she stepped out of the room. Resting her head back against the pillow, Georgie met her mother's eyes, glossy with unshed tears, as she reached for her other hand.

"I love you, Mom," Georgie managed to croak out, her throat dry and sore.

Her mother wiped a rogue tear from her cheek and smiled, "I love you too, my dear sweet, brave girl. I'm going to leave you and Brooks to talk and go text everyone that you're awake."

With a last squeeze of her hand, Georgie's gaze followed her mother as she left the room, her eyes drifting over to Brooks, who sat on the edge of her bed, his hand still holding hers.

"The doctor said everything went smoothly with no complications, and it should take four to six weeks to heal," he said, glancing down at the bandage around her chest and torso.

Georgie frowned as she tried to look down to see what

he was seeing, but the pain was too much, and she let her head fall back onto the pillow. "I guess I won't need a bra anymore."

"I guess not," he said, meeting her eyes, a sparkle of mischief in his gaze. "What is the German word for bra? Georgie's lips tugged up in a weary smile. "Stopemfrom-floppen."

A faint giggle escaped her throat, followed by a wince as the pain in her chest surged.

"Sorry," he said, frowning with care. "I guess jokes aren't a good idea right now."

Georgie squeezed his hand, a small smile curving her lips. "I love you, Brooks. Jokes and all."

* * *

THE SUMMER SUN outside cast shadows on the wall of their bedroom. Bands of light danced as Georgie woke herself from a deep sleep with a long-drawn-out moan. A rough scruff tickled her thighs as Brooks licked, sucked, and teased at her core.

"Brooks," she breathed out as her fingers feathered through his curly hair, pulling it as she shamelessly rocked against his mouth. "You are far too good at this."

Lifting his head, he gave her a devilish grin. "I aim to please," he said as he spread her wider and hungrily coaxed her to climax. Body shaking with aftershocks, Brooks kissed a trail of passionate kisses up her body, lifting her shirt as he kissed up her stomach to her chest.

"Brooks, no." Georgie scolded, pulling her nightshirt back down, covering where her breasts once were, and dark thick scars formed in their place. Glancing away, Georgie wrapped her arms tightly around her chest, with Brooks hovering above her as tears formed in her eyes and she whispered roughly, "It's ugly."

"Look at me, Georgie."

Turning, her eyes met his gaze, soft and compassionate. "We all have scars, Georgie. I could point out at least a dozen on my body right now. Some are large and some are small, but they are all a part of me, Georgie. Just like your scars are now a part of you. Scars are just reminders that you are stronger than what tried to hurt you. They don't change how beautiful and special you are. They're just a reminder that you survived," he implored her with his loving gaze. "To me, that makes them beautiful. So, no more hiding them. Let me love every inch of you."

Georgie blinked away the tears as she swallowed down the emotion and slowly unwrapped her arms from her chest, allowing him to lift her shirt and reveal herself to him.

Brooks' eyes raked over her body reverently before letting his eyes drift up to meet hers. "So beautiful." He said as he lowered his lips to her chest and kissed along the line of the scar, first on one side and then the other.

Closing her eyes, Georgie sighed, savoring the feel of his soft, sensual kisses across her skin. "I want you inside me," she breathed out, pulling his head up to brand him with a scorching kiss.

Brooks reached over to the nightstand, and she stopped him, his eyes flitting to hers in question. "No barriers, please, Brooks. I want to feel all of you."

"Is that a good idea?" he asked, his brows drawing together as he searched her eyes.

"I don't care if it is or not. I need this first with you," she replied, brushing the curls from his eyes.

"Beautiful, what if you get pregnant? It's only been six months since your last chemo treatment." He reasoned. "Have you talked to your doctor and oncologist about a pregnancy post-chemo? I read that getting pregnant while the drugs are still in your system could cause birth defects."

"Since when have you become an expert on post-cancer fertility?" Georgie asked, pinning him with a glare.

"I've done some reading," he replied. "Once your body returns to regular cycles, there is a possibility that you could get pregnant, but likely we will need to get referred to a fertility specialist."

"And that's what you want? A baby created in a doctor's office, by some lab technician, possibly not even a part of me as I can't produce any eggs. With a donor egg?"

"If that's what we need to do, yes. There's nothing wrong with fertility treatment. Jaxon and Dee went through it, and they now have a family."

"Their situation is very different, Brooks, and you know that," she said, pushing at his chest to attempt to create distance between them.

Brooks lifted off her and gave her a confused look. "I know it's very different, but why wouldn't we investigate every option?"

Georgie felt agitation rise in her body as she reached for her sleep shirt and sat up, slipping it back on, closing her eyes and taking a deep breath before she answered. "I have no problem with fertility treatment or exploring our options, Brooks. But I dream of the moment when I hold that positive pregnancy test in my hand with you beside me, overjoyed at the surprise of knowing we created a life together. Just us. No test tubes or, God forbid, more drugs. Just you and I naturally conceiving a child that is a little of me and a little of you. That's what I want, Brooks," she explained as she shifted and rose from the bed, her voice cracking. Facing away from him, she took a deep breath and let it out in a long-pained exhale before she turned, to be met by his eyes, a combination of sadness and bewilderment in their depths. "And I likely will never be able to have that. To give you and us that. I will never be able to know what that kind of joy is like, and it's eating me up inside, worse than the fucking cancer."

"Georgie..." Brooks started, but Georgie cut him off.

"I'm going to go take a shower. I have therapy sessions today, and I'm going to be late if I don't get moving," she said with a shaky voice as she turned and strode towards the bathroom, leaving Brooks behind speechless.

GEORGIE WAITED in her doctor's office, eyes drifting over the same pictures and certificates that graced the exam room walls. Her eyes zoned in on one that she hadn't seen before, her doctor, with two little girls on her lap, dressed in pretty pink sundresses, their soft waves of dark brown hair pinned at the sides with sparkly clips, a handsome dark-haired man standing behind them, smiling proudly. Her family.

The exam room door opened, and her doctor entered, offering her a bright smile as she took a seat at the desk, set down her chart and clicked around on her computer before turning to face her, clapping her hands together.

"Georgie, it's so good to see you again. How are you feeling?" she asked, her brown eyes reflecting deep sincerity with her question.

"I'm good. My energy is coming back, which is nice. I finally feel well enough to ride again." Georgie replied with a half-smile.

"Well, that's positive. Getting your energy back is half the battle. How is your mental health? I know you're a professional in this area, so I feel I can be candid with you. Have you been experiencing any depression or general feelings of hopelessness? Your body has been through a lot, but your mind has also been through the wringer. How are you doing in that respect?"

"I have good days and bad days. Mostly grappling with my body image and uncertainty as to what the future holds for me." Georgie replied honestly.

"Can you elaborate on that? What about the future is causing you some trepidation?" the doctor asked, concern edging her voice.

"I've always dreamt of being a mother, and I'm scared that it's no longer a possibility."

Her doctor turned to the screen in front of her and clicked around a few times, bringing her gaze back to Georgie.

"You know that door isn't closed, Georgie. It's hard for

me to say as a general practitioner whether you'll be able to conceive and carry a child naturally, but there are options, and with your age, that will be an advantage to you. It really does depend on how long your oncologist wants you to continue the post-chemo medication and whether your final scans come back clear."

"But my cycles haven't returned, and it's been seven months since my last treatment." Georgie replied. "What if they never return?"

"I'm not going to say it's not a possibility, but right now you're still in a timeline that is acceptable for your body's regular functions to still be delayed. And if it never does return to normal, it doesn't mean that you don't have options to become a parent. Science has made miraculous strides in fertility, then there is surrogacy or adoption."

"I honestly don't want to even consider other options right now. I only want to carry a child myself." Georgie said with conviction. "And I know that may come across as selfish, but it's something I've dreamt of my entire life, and I don't want to settle.

"I get it, Georgie," she replied, picking up a picture on her desk and smiling down at it before she handed it to Georgie. Georgie took the picture, a close-up of the two pretty little girls from the family photo on the wall. "These are my daughters, Brooklyn and Paige. My husband and I adopted them five years ago after over a decade of fertility treatments that never worked for us. We exhausted every possible option, and I remember feeling like I had failed us. And then, a friend of mine, who is a social worker here in St. Augustine, brought up adoption. The more I looked into it, the more it called to me, and less than a year later, my girls, two years old and nine months old at the time, were placed with us."

"Did you feel like you were their mother?" Georgie asked, genuinely curious.

"Instantly," her doctor replied without hesitation. Georgie smoothed her hand over the picture, smiled and handed it back to her doctor, meeting her eyes. "My advice to you is to be open to every possibility, Georgie. What is meant to be, is meant to be."

Georgie took in those words, letting them sink in. She would be a mother someday. There was no question that she was called to be one, but she wasn't going to give up on being the one to carry a child of her own. Not until her very last breath.

CHAPTER 14

$\mathcal{E}$arly onset menopause caused by chemotherapy. Those words made her heart fall into the pit of her stomach. After speaking to her doctor, she was referred to a fertility specialist who, after blood work, an ultrasound, and after analyzing a series of continued symptoms, determined the diagnosis. Georgie walked out of the clinic office, her hand in Brooks, the silence between them thick and her throat painfully tight, constricting her breathing. Reaching his truck, Georgie didn't wait for him to open her door, simply climbed in and buckled her seat belt, settling her hands in her lap, no words able to formulate in her head.

Brooks climbed into the cab, his eyes drifting over to hers, his mouth in a grim line as he reached over and placed his hand over hers. "It doesn't mean we can't become parents, Georgie."

She nodded and turned, resting her head against the cold glass of the passenger-side window. Her breath swirled in front of her as she tried to breathe in and out, the warmth of her breath causing a thin layer of conden-sation to form on the inside of the window. She closed her eyes, suddenly feeling tired. So achingly tired that she wanted to sleep forever and get lost in the dreams she had for her life, which were slowly slipping through her fingers.

* * *

BROOKS RAN his hand through his hair, lowering his head and pulling at the curls painfully. Georgie hadn't left their room in weeks, barely having eaten the food that he brought upstairs for her or having left their bed. She lay there, engulfed in his large Johnny Cash T-shirt, her stare blank, and eyes swollen and red-rimmed from sobbing.

Concern, fear, every emotion hit him all at once as he sat there lost and completely unsure of how to help her. The deep chasm of depression she had fallen into was far beyond his scope, and he needed help.

A knock sounded at the door, and Brooks rose from the table, wiping the hopeless tears that trailed down his face away as he strode to the front door. Opening the door, Emmaline Donahue and his mother, Dorothy Isley, stood there, their eyes full of love and compassion as they wrapped their arms around Brooks and hugged him tightly. A long-pained exhale escaped as they clung to him, and more tears rolled down his cheeks as he gave in to the anguish of the situation. He needed this hug. The hug from two women who had seen him grow up, had been there since the beginning and had foreseen his future with Georgie. *If there is still a future to be had.*

"Brooks, honey, it's all going to be okay," his mother cooed, rubbing his back as they entered the house.

"I don't know what to do anymore," he replied, worry, fear and exhaustion hitting him all at once. "It's like she's given up on life." The three took a seat at the kitchen table, Brooks glancing between them both. "She's hardly gotten out of bed since our appointment at the fertility specialist. She's hardly eaten, has only drunk, which is a small victory, and I honesly don't know how often she's showered."

"Sounds like depression," Emmaline replied, shaking her head.

"What did the specialist say that caused her to react this way?" Brooks' mother questioned.

"That the chemo has put her into early menopause and that having kids naturally may not be in the cards for us," he replied.

"And are you open to other options to become parents?" his mother asked.

"Of course. I honestly am open to anything, but Georgie..." he trailed off, shaking his head. "I understand the disappointment. I would be lying if I said I wasn't a little, but I'm just happy we know now and can look forward to and pursue other avenues to have children."

Both mothers nodded their heads, Emmaline cocking her eyebrow in challenge. "Alright, it's time for Operation Tough Love to step in. First order of operations: get my daughter out of bed and into a shower or bath. You, Brooks, stay down here and make her something simple to eat. Something she can't resist, and if we need your muscle, we'll call for you, got it?"

Brooks nodded, an unexpected chuckle finding its way through the tears, with both mothers rising from the table, looks of determination in their eyes as they marched up the stairs to their bedroom.

* * *

GEORGIE HEARD THE KNOCK DOWNSTAIRS, the murmur of voices, but nothing more. The cocoon of protection she had surrounded herself with was impenetrable from the outside world. A place she was safe. A place devoid of people, a place devoid of judgment, a place devoid of sympathetic looks. A place she could lay quietly and stew in her mourning.

Hearing the specialist say that conceiving would likely never happen for her felt like the last kick in the teeth. One last blow to her pride and existence. Cancer had robbed her of so much, and now it had taken away the last thing she had wished for, a family. And worse, it had taken it away from Brooks. Brooks was born to be a father, and he deserved to be one. He wanted to marry her, but would he resent her in the end if he did? Would he in the long-term regret choosing her despite their friendship and years of history together?

The sound of footsteps on the stairs broke Georgie from her thoughts as the bedroom door opened, and she lifted her head off the pillow to see both her own and Brooks' mother standing at the foot of the bed, their hands on their hips.

"Georgie, it's time you got out of this bed and into a bath. You're not going to sit here and wallow in self-pity.

The pity party is over." Her mother declared firmly as she pulled on the comforter, uncovering her in the process.

"Mom," Georgie whimpered, giving her mother a disbelieving look.

"Dorothy, can you go draw Georgie a bath, please?" She said to Brooks mom, her friend complying with her request. "I want to talk to my daughter alone for a moment."

Georgie sat up, leaning against the headboard, her arms wrapped around her legs, much like she did as a little girl when she felt uncomfortable or when she was being scolded for something she did or said. Her parents weren't strict, but they weren't pushovers either, and Georgie was headstrong, so it wasn't uncommon for her to be the recipient of a lecture.

Her mother gave her a compassionate look and took a seat on the edge of the bed, turning to face her.

"Georgie, sweetheart. You've been dealt a shitty hand, and I know it sucks. But you can't shut yourself off from everything good in your life. You have a job you love, family and friends who love and adore you, and a man downstairs who loves you so much he called me and his mother in to set you straight. Even if you can't see it right now, Georgie, you are so blessed." She said, offering her a comforting smile as she rose from the bed and put out her hand. "It's time to start living again. Start focussing on what you have instead of what you won't. C'mon, let's get out of this bed and into a bath. Once you feel refreshed, we're going to go downstairs and you're going to eat something. Understand?"

Georgie stared at her mother a few beats; their determined gazes locked. There was no way her mother was going to concede. Her stubbornness a trait she passed onto Georgie.

"C'mon Georgie. You have a choice here. Wallow or start living again."

Defeated, tears formed in Georgie's eyes at her mother's words because if those were the choices, there was only one that made sense. The choice she had made when she was diagnosed with cancer. To live. Georgie blinked, tears falling down her face as she nodded, accepting her mother's hand as she shuffled off the bed and rose to her feet, her legs wobbly, her body weak. The neglect of her needs having taken a toll on her body, her mother wrapped her arm around her waist, holding her up as they slowly made their way into the bathroom.

Brooks mother was there, lavender bubble bath in hand. As her eyes met Georgie's, so full of love and compassion for her as she said, "Your bath is ready, sweetheart. I'll be downstairs with my son."

With just her and her mother in the room, Georgie let her mother undress her, just as she had done when she was a little girl, and helped her step into the tub. As Georgie let the soothing heat of the water envelope her, she sighed as her mother reached for a sponge and she leaned forward, letting her mother tenderly wash her back. A deep silence fell on them both as Georgie's mother bathed her and then washed her hair, massaging the shampoo into her scalp. Surrendering to her mother's loving touch, Georgie closed her eyes, and tried to focus on breathing. *In and out. In and out. When was the last time you just breathed?*

"Let me get you a fresh towel." Her mother said as the water started to cool. Slipping out of the room, Georgie, now alone, inhaled a deep shuddering breath, and exhaled slowly, her mind starting to clear from the fog. Her mother returned and helped her climb out of the tub, her mother wrapping the towel around her and leading her into the bedroom where she laid out pajamas on the bed. "Do you want my help, or can you get dressed on your own?"

"I'll never have a baby." Georgie whispered, feeling a wave of emotion rise in her chest as she met her mother's gaze.

Her mother reached out and caressed her face. "I know, sweetheart," she said, searching her eyes. "But you will be a mother. Somehow, some way you will experience what it's like to love a child that was destined to be yours." Georgie nodded, giving her mother a half smile. "This is the path you've been given, Georgie, now you need to walk down it and embrace it." She said as a wistful look washed across her face. "Do you remember what you said to me after your father passed away?" Georgie shook her head. "You told me that even though life gives us lemons, we have to get up and make fucking lemonade."

A giggle escaped, and Georgie covered her mouth as she replied, "Mom, you don't swear."

"Well, there's a first time for everything." Her mother replied with a playful smile. "That advice got me out of my funk. It brought me out of my place of mourning and got me moving again. You're probably going to mourn this dream for a while, but don't sit in this space too long.

You have a wedding and a whole life full of love with Brooks to look forward to."

Georgie nodded as tears pricked her eyes, but for the first time in a long time, they weren't tears of sorrow, but tears of hope.

* * *

THE FIRE CRACKLED in the firepit. The chilly late September night brought with it a promise of colder weather ahead. Brooks threw two more logs on the fire and walked over to Georgie, curled up on an Adirondack chair with a large blanket draped over her shoulders. He smiled, his blue eyes dancing with the flicker of the bonfire flames as he picked her up in one swoop and settled into the chair, cradling her in his lap. Georgie snuggled into him, her head resting on his shoulder as they watched the embers rise into the night sky.

"Are you feeling better?" he asked, his fingers playing with her chin-length waves of hair.

Their mothers had left two hours ago after they were certain Georgie wouldn't drift back into the pitiful state she had been in, had eaten and had contacted a therapist colleague to make an appointment. Those women were a force, and he was beyond grateful to them.

"I will be," she replied, glancing up and meeting his gaze. "It'll take some time to get there, but I will, I promise you that. I guess one thing that keeps troubling me is how this is going to affect you. I know you say you're okay with it, not having a child of your own, but will you wake up one day and resent that you chose me?"

Brooks shifted, turning his head so he could stare into her eyes straight on. Georgie's eyes reflected her fears, and he brought his hand up, smoothing away the tendrils of soft waves from her forehead and tucked them behind her ear. Caressing her cheek, she leaned into him as unshed tears made her eyes shine in the light of the fire. "I promise I will always choose you, Georgie. I truly believe from the depths of my soul that we were destined to be together. Call it fate, call it magic, call it whatever you want, but I believe you were put on this earth to be my best friend, my lover, and my wife. We are each other's soulmates. It's as simple and as complicated as that."

Georgie smiled, her head touching his as they breathed together, eyes closed, reveling in his words and promises. "I want to marry you, Brooks, but I need to get my head on straight before I do. Are you okay with waiting just a little longer?"

He lifted his head from hers and replied, "I will wait forever if that's what it takes."

"Thank you for loving me through all of this," she said, eyes locked on his as she ran her hands through his curly hair.

Brooks smiled, bringing his lips to hers and pausing as they breathed the same air. "Till my last breath, Georgie. I will always love you."

CHAPTER 15

As fall turned to winter and the snow melted with the spring rain, Georgie felt lighter, more effervescent than she had in a long time. Brooks continued to love her through all her extreme ups and downs. He was there to take her to her therapy appointments and even joined in when requested. He held her when she needed to cry after Kolt and Jane announced their second pregnancy and, despite being happy for them, felt sad for what she was missing out on. He was there cheering and clapping louder than her doctors and the nurses combined when she rang the bell at the cancer treatment centre, signifying she was finally cancer-free. He was there, solid, and unwavering. Her mighty oak protected her and kept her grounded to the earth and this beautiful life they were creating together.

Coming out of the ensuite, Brooks was propped against the headboard, shirtless, his curly hair damp and sexily disheveled from his shower, his facial scruff longer than usual making him look like a rugged mountain man as he read her latest romance novel.

"You know, this sexy smut you read is giving me all sorts of wicked ideas," he said, his eyes meeting hers as he waggled his eyebrows.

"Is that so?" she replied as she climbed over him and straddled his lap.

His large hands slid over her waist and hips before settling on her behind pulling her closer. Feeling the hard ridge of him start to tent his cotton sleep pants, she rocked on top of him, making his eyes grow darker with lust.

"I'm ready." she breathed out, her own arousal sizzling low in her belly.

"So am I." he replied, snarling as he nibbled on her neck.

Georgie let out a little giggle as she pulled away and explained, "I'm ready to get married."

Brooks' eyes morphed from carnal lust to questioning as he cupped her face with both hands, searching her gaze. "Are you being serious right now?"

"Yes, I want to get married. This spring. As soon as possible if we can," she declared with a huge smile.

"I can check with Falyn to see when she would have the bed-and-breakfast available, and we can book a date." he replied, his handsome smile growing wider.

Georgie nodded as an idea popped into her head and her lips curled up in a smile. "Check with her about the reception afterwards; I have another idea for the ceremony."

* * *

WITH THE DATE SET, Brooks and Georgie invited all their friends and family to the ceremony. No formal invitations were sent out, just a social media group created with instructions to check the group one hour before the ceremony for a pinned map guiding them to the ceremony location. When their family and friends would question where the ceremony was to be, their only answer was it was a secret and to wait for instructions.

"I don't understand why you need to be so cryptic about where you're getting married, Georgie," her mother asked, brows drawn together as she glanced at Georgie in her full-length mirror and adjusted the skirt on Georgie's wedding dress. Meeting her gaze, she preened, "You look so beautiful, Sweetheart. This dress was made for you."

Georgie beamed at her mother and looked down at the pretty, scalloped-neck satin gown, with Juliet sleeves, fitted bodice and full skirt of satin and tulle. It was her mother's wedding dress, and when she asked if she could wear it for their wedding, her mother was so overcome by her request that she wept. Georgie dabbed at her face, a tear escaping the corner of her eye at the memory and instantly missing her father. "I wish Dad was here." Georgie said, sniffing back tears.

"He's here in spirit." Her mother said, reaching up and catching a tear of her own. "Your dad wanted this for you. To marry someone who loved all of you and made you truly happy. He adored Brooks. I'm sure he's looking down on you right now, so proud of the woman you've become. I know I'm proud."

Georgie gave her mother a wistful smile as she pulled her in for a hug. "I love you, Mom."

"I love you too, sweetheart."

Suddenly Georgie's phone vibrated on the dresser, and she smiled, knowing it was Brooks. Striding over, she picked up her phone and smiled at the text he sent.

Brooks: The location has been revealed, and the comments are flying. Everyone is confused. It's hilarious. In just over an hour, you're going to be Mrs. Isley. Are you excited, Beautiful?

Georgie: Beyond.

Brooks: See you at our place. I'll be the guy in the dapper tuxedo.

Georgie: And I'll be the girl in the dress ready to marry the man of my dreams.

Brooks: You, Georgie, are my dream. Always have been, always will be. I love you.

Georgie: I love you too.

Georgie set down her phone and turned to her mother. "The location has been posted. I can finish getting ready on my own. I'll see you there."

"Are you sure?" her mother asked, her face a mixture of hesitation and bewilderment.

"Yes!" Georgie exclaimed as her brother, Kolt, peeked into the bedroom. His eyes landed on Georgie, and his face brightened with a wide smile.

"Georgie, you look amazing. Wait till you see Brooks..." his eyes gleamed. "You are going to howl."

Georgie clapped her hands and let out a little squeal of excitement.

Her mother simply laughed, shook her head, and gave Georgie a quick kiss on the cheek as she left with Kolt, who was to deliver her to the ceremony site.

Alone, Georgie took one last look at her reflection and reached for the crown of colorful flowers on her bed. Setting it on her head, she smiled, feeling a lightness in her chest and a flutter in her heart. Today was the beginning of the rest of her life with Brooks, and she couldn't wait for this new chapter to begin.

* * *

BROOKS PACED the front walkway at his parent's house, unable to stay still. It was 30 minutes until the ceremony, and in 15 minutes he was to make his way to the ceremony site. Every single minute had been thought out and choreographed, and he couldn't wait to see Georgie. Reaching into the inside pocket of his rented vintage tuxedo, he pulled out the piece of paper he had slipped in there earlier. Unfolding the paper, he read through his words, his declarations to Georgie; everything he wanted to say spilled out onto the page. His hands trembled, an inadvertent reaction to his pulse racing with anticipation at seeing his beautiful bride.

Today was a day he always hoped would happen, but never dared to dream that it would. Each and every memory of the two of them played back so vividly in his mind as emotion rose in his chest and his throat grew thick. Closing his eyes, he took a deep cleansing breath as he steadied his emotions. *Save the tears for the ceremony, Isley.* His watch beeped, signaling 15 minutes till showtime. With one deep cleansing breath, he walked over to his bicycle, climbed aloft it, pedaled down the driveway to the gravel road and turned towards his destination.

GEORGIE PEDALED HARD, her dress bunched up awkwardly and tucked strategically so it wouldn't get damaged or caught in the spokes of the bicycle wheels. Off in the distance, a long caravan of vehicles was parked along the two gravel roads as guests gathered at the intersection. Their intersection. Their secret place where two prairie roads meet. Georgie let out a little giggle, thinking about what their family and friends must be thinking as they stood there, perplexed, on the dusty country road. She glanced across the corner of the field, seeing Brooks off in the distance, likely pedalling as hard as she was. He was a flash of baby blue, and she laughed, thinking about how epic he must look in his vintage 80s-inspired tuxedo.

Drawing closer, she heard "Eye of the Tiger" blasting from portable speakers set up at the ceremony site and she smiled as she dug her heels into the pedals to go faster with Brooks drawing closer and doing the same. Their guests faces a combination of pure mirth and in some cases utter confusion. As they drew nearer to them, the bountiful mix of laughter, catcalls, clapping, cheering and hoots and hollers surrounding them in the open air. Georgie waved and glanced over at Brooks, who had just arrived ahead of her, fixing the kickstand of his bicycle and turning as she drove up beside him and carefully climbed off her bicycle. Handing her bicycle to Kolt,

Brooks took her hand, his eyes meeting hers, then roaming over her with appreciation.

"You are perfect," he smiled. "More beautiful than I imagined."

Georgie drew closer, looking up at him through her long lashes as she smoothed her hand over the satin of his lapel and straightened out his matching satin bow tie. "And you look like a dream. This was the best idea ever, wasn't it?"

"Damn straight it was," he said with a wink as he took her hand. "Shall we get married, Beautiful?" he asked, gesturing to the makeshift aisle Falyn had set up for them. The aisle consisted of a pink roll-out carpet leading to a vintage white wicker trellis Georgie found at a thrift store that was covered by colorful flowers that matched her flower crown.

Falyn handed Georgie a simple bouquet, and she returned her gaze back to Brooks. "Let's do this."

"Time After Time" by Cyndi Lauper started to play, as hand in hand, Brooks and Georgie walked down the aisle, fielding greetings and smiles from guests as they slowly walked towards the trellis, where Mr. Estes, the local Marriage Commissioner, stood. He smirked as he looked between them, and the music faded.

"Welcome, friends and family, to this joyous wedding ceremony for Georgette Donahue and Brooks Isley. I've had the privilege of marrying many couples in and around Primrose, and I've even married a couple in the middle of a field on a utility road." He said, glancing around until his eyes met Hayden and Whitney Hastings, who beamed from the sidelines, their arms around each other's waists. "I've had the joy of bringing so many incredible couples together, and I feel beyond privileged to be able to marry Brooks and Georgie today here at this juncture of two prairie roads, that as I understand holds deep significance to them both."

Brooks glanced at Georgie, and she grinned up at him as she squeezed his hand.

"So, let's get these two hitched, shall we?" Mr. Estes said with a wink. "Brooks, how about we start with you?"

Brooks took a sharp inhale and exhaled slowly as he reached into his jacket pocket to pull out his vows. Opening the paper slowly, his hands trembled as he met her eyes, his blue eyes sparkling in the sun as he flashed her a playful grin and wiped a rogue tear from the corner of his eye as he asked, "What do you call tears on your wedding day?" Georgie giggled and shrugged. "Eye Dew."

Laughter and jeers rose behind them, and Brooks' eyes darted around their guests as he shouted, "You know I had to!" followed by more laughter. He returned his gaze to Georgie, with so much love in his eyes as he continued. "Georgie, I have loved you for as long as I can remember. If I tried to pinpoint the exact moment, I knew how I felt about you, I'm not sure I could. It was a culmination of the countless hours, reading, laughing, talking, spending time together sharing our every thought, hope and dream. This is where you became my best friend, confidante and somewhere in the mix of all of it I fell in love with you. A million memories shared right here in our secret place. Which I guess is no longer a secret!" he exclaimed, glancing around at their smiling guests as he let out a chuckle through his tears. His eyes drifted back to

Georgie's as he let out a puff of air to steady his emotions and continued, his voice breaking with his continued words. "Not so long ago, I was scared I was going to lose you." Georgie swallowed hard, her brows knit together as her own tears started, and she reached up and caressed his cheek. "Watching you fight. Fight for your life and fight for our future, if you can believe it, made me love you more. Georgie, you are, in one word, remarkable, and I'm honored that you've chosen me. You are the love of my life, and I will spend the rest of my life doing everything in my power to make all your dreams come true."

Georgie wiped at the tears on her face as Brooks reached into his pocket and produced two handkerchiefs, one for her and one for him. They both laughed as they wiped their tears and blew their noses. Many of their emotional guests followed suit.

Mr. Estes dabbed at his own face and gestured for Georgie to go ahead.

Taking a deep breath and letting it out slowly, Georgie met Brooks gaze, her heart feeling full to bursting as she looked up at the man she loved. Her best friend, lover and the man who stood by her unfailingly through the most difficult time of her life. *How do I properly express what he means to me? Are there words poignant enough?*

"Brooks, I heard once that real love doesn't meet you at your best. It meets you in your mess. I spent years searching for the right one, wishing a white knight would ride into town and sweep me off my feet. It took me being faced with my own mortality to finally see that my white knight was right in front of me all the time." Georgie's chin quivered, and she swallowed down, trying to steady her emotions as she continued, "Brooks, every single road led me straight to you. A path I was always meant to take, even if I took a few detours along the way. You, Brooks, are my north, my south, my east, and my west. You have been my compass, guiding me through all the challenges and mess of the past two years. You are my best friend and the love of my life," she said, beaming up at him. "I promise to stand by you, support you and remind you every day that I choose you. I love you, Brooksy."

"I love you too, Georgie. So much."

Mr. Estes stepped forward. "Rings?"

Kolt stepped forward and handed them to Mr. Estes, who handed a simple gold band to Brooks. "I Brooks, take you, Georgie, to be my wife. I vow to face all of life's triumphs and challenges with you, and no matter where the road of life may lead us, I promise to walk beside you for the rest of our lives." Brooks said as he placed the ring on her finger.

Taking the second ring, Georgie vowed, "I Georgie, take you, Brooks, to be my husband. I vow to face all of life's triumphs and challenges with you, and no matter where the road of life leads us, I promise to walk beside you for the rest of our lives." With those words, she slipped the band onto Brooks's finger.

"Do you, Brooks Isley, take Georgie Donahue to be your wife?"

"Hell, yeah, I do!" he exclaimed, followed by a swell of tearful laughter from their guests.

"And do you Georgie Donahue, take Brooks Isley to be your husband?"

"I do too!" she exclaimed.

"Then by the power vested in me by the province of Manitoba, I now pronounce you married. Brooks, you may kiss your bride."

Georgie hooked her arms around his neck, and he lifted her, her legs dangling as they stared deep into each other's eyes. "Well, Big guy, you're my husband.

"I'm your husband."

"Are you going to kiss me?" Georgie asked with a giggle, her cheek dipping into the dimple Brooks loved so much as she threaded her fingers through his curly hair.

Brooks gazed into her beautiful brown eyes. The eyes of the woman he loved more than life itself as he replied, "Every single day, for the rest of our lives." Lowering his lips to hers, he kissed her, the page turning in their love story and their happily ever after awaiting.

* * *

GLANCING around the yard of Prairie Charm Bed and Breakfast, Brooks took in all their friends and family, visiting, laughing, and partaking in the incredible food Falyn had prepared for the event. Everyone enjoying the fellowship of simply being together. Brooks felt emotion rise in his chest as he thought about how the community had come out for them. Everyone they knew and loved gathered at the dusty corner of two prairie roads to witness the love he and Georgie shared. All of those that supported them, big and small, through the challenges of the past two years and never asked for anything in return. This was a community. This was Primrose.

"Hey there, Big Guy," the sweet voice of his wife

said as he turned to see Georgie strolling up to him. She wrapped her arms around his waist, and he leaned down, brushing his lips to hers. She purred softly against his lips, and he deepened their kiss, not caring who was watching. Pulling away, Georgie stared up at him dreamily. "This has been a magical day."

"And we'll have a magical life," he replied.

"As long as you're by my side, I have no doubt it will be," she said, giving him an affectionate squeeze as she gazed up at him lovingly.

"So, what's next, Mrs. Isley?" Brooks asked as he stared deep into the eyes of his beautiful bride.

Georgie tapped her chin and met him with a conspiring smile. "I think I'd like to get a dog."

"A dog?" he questioned in surprise as a slow smile curled his lips. "I like that idea. What else?"

"Perhaps a bigger house, something big enough so we can fill it." She replied, biting her bottom lip as she met his inquiring gaze.

"Oh, does this mean you've made a decision about having a family?" he asked, raising his eyebrow in a question.

She nodded, "I want to adopt, Brooks. And build a big, beautiful family with you. I know I've been set on having a child of our own, but I think this is God's plan for us. And any child we bring into our family is going to be a blessing."

A rush of love filled Brooks heart at the confirming words he longed to hear from Georgie. Enveloping her in his arms, he closed his eyes, relishing the feel of her fitting perfectly in his hold and eager to see what the future had in store.

Brooks' favouite song blasted from the speakers, and cheers swelled from their guests as the dance floor emptied, making way for what was sure to be a show.

"Dance with me, my sexy wife," he said as he dragged her over to the floor. "You're an Isley now, and if there is one thing we know how to do, it's dance."

Georgie rolled her eyes as Brooks started his strut and gestured for her to walk the catwalk with him. Obliging they strutted, wiggled, posed, and laughed until their sides hurt as everyone they loved joined them on the dance floor.

Brooks' heart felt full. Full of love, promise and hope for the future. He was certain that they would have difficulties ahead. More challenges that simply living would bring them. But now as he twirled the one and only woman he ever loved, her face flushed with pure joy and folly as she giggled, her eyes sparkled under the fairy lights, he knew without a doubt that with Georgie by his side, they could get through anything.

EPILOGUE

Five years later

Georgie sat on their back deck overlooking the horse pasture and little barn off to the side of the house, nursing a cup of tea as she watched Brooks and their girls play with their golden retriever, Gus. It had been two years since they had built their home on the property her father had gifted her. She loved living here, close to family, her work and the town she loved so much.

Six years post cancer Georgie remained in remission, those difficult days of anxiety and uncertainty now a distant memory. She felt good, had returned to her regular workload, despite life having gotten busier after adopting their girls. Three years ago, she and Brooks were contacted by their social worker with the news that two little girls needed a home, Evelyn, three years old, and her little sister, Emma, who was only a year old. Two little girls who recently lost their mother to cancer and had no other family to speak of. When they got word that the girl's' mother chose them, Georgie took it as a sign. A sign that this was God's plan all along. The moment she laid eyes on her two beautiful little girls, she was in love. Not a single day went by, where she didn't feel like their mother, and although becoming an instant family wasn't easy, Georgie felt immeasurably blessed to have them come into her life.

As for Brooks, he fell into his role as a father seamlessly. The girls adored him from day one, and being a girl dad suited him perfectly. He would play dress up with them, hold tea parties, and seeing her big oaf of a husband wearing a tutu and a tiara may have been the highlight of her life. But her favorite part about seeing him as a father was those quiet moments when they were all snuggled on the couch watching movies or when she would watch from the rocking chair as he would read them bedtime stories, always making up funny voices for the characters like he did when they were kids.

Although life was hectic, with daycare, packing lunches and snacks, dance lessons and community sports, Georgie wouldn't have changed it for the world. All those years of worry about the future were now in the rear-view mirror, and thinking back to all that time she wasted fighting with herself and questioning if pursuing her attraction to Brooks would affect their friendship felt silly now. Brooks was still her best friend, their friendship the best foundation for their marriage, and Georgie was grateful every day that she had finally listened to her heart.

"Hey there, Beautiful." Brooks said, climbing the stairs

to the back deck and joining her at the patio table. His round face was flushed and sweaty, and he had little bits of grass stuck in his curly hair. Georgie laughed as he shook his head, letting the grass land on her before he leaned down, kissed her tenderly and took a seat beside her. "How are you feeling?"

"Tired, and my stomach still isn't right. I think I need to make an appointment with my doctor." She said with a deep sigh. Although Georgie was cancer free, she was cautious and never felt like her immunity had returned fully after the chemo. Having two young daughters in school, they picked up every illness that rotated through their classrooms, and she wasn't about to take chances with her health.

"Do you think you'll be okay to go to Gatton's birthday party this afternoon?" Brooks asked, reaching for her hand. "I can always take the girls if you want to stay home and rest. And I'm sure everyone will understand."

"No, I should be fine." She replied, shaking her head. "I wouldn't miss this party for the world."

ARRIVING at Kolt and Jane's farm, they found the driveway was already full of vehicles. Pulling open the side door of the minivan, Brooks helped the girls out while Georgie retrieved their gift for Gatton. Kids were running amok everywhere; lawn chairs dappled the yard with friends and family visiting, and a long table was set up in the shade with salads and munchies. The smell of the barbecue wafted through the yard, and as the smell hit Georgie's nose, her stomach did a nauseous flip-flop.

"I'm going to go inside to find Jane," Georgie said, not wanting to alarm Brooks with her incessant stomach issues.

"Okay, I'll watch over the kiddos, and you have fun catching up with the girls," he said as he gave her hand a squeeze and let go.

She feigned a smile and climbed the porch stairs to the front door. Walking inside and letting the storm door slam behind her, Georgie spotted Jane at the kitchen island with Falyn, her two-year-old daughter, Abigail, balanced on her hip and a decorating bag in her one free hand. Georgie set down the gift on the kitchen table and said, "Let me take Abby while you finish up those cupcakes."

Jane gave her a grateful look as she handed the toddler to Georgie. Georgie sat down on a stool by the kitchen island, perching Abby on the countertop and tickling her side, making her squirm and giggle. She loved her nephews and niece, and now living just a mile from each other; she got to spend as much time as she wanted with them.

Jane continued to decorate the cupcakes, Falyn helping, and Georgie couldn't help but notice how exhausted she looked, which wasn't uncommon for her with three rambunctious kids, yet today she looked even more so.

"Are you okay, Jane?" Georgie asked, her brows drawn together in concern. "Please don't tell me you have that nasty flu that's going around. I just got over being sick, and my stomach still isn't 100% right."

A smile tugged at Jane's lips as she leaned in, glancing between Falyn and Georgie. "I'm pregnant." She said in a low tone. Falyn beamed, and Georgie was ready to let out a delighted squeal when Jane gestured for them to keep it down. "I only took a test this morning, and Kolt doesn't know yet. I plan on telling him after the kids are in bed tonight."

"I'm so excited for you, Jane," Georgie said. "Yikes though, four kids under the age of ten."

"I know." Jane replied as she picked up the decorator bag again and sighed. "Darn sexy cowboy husband." Both Falyn and Georgie laughed as she continued, "I actually thought I had caught the flu that seems to be running wild through the school. But I was just so tired and felt nauseous all the time. The usual food triggers and smells bothered me just like with the last three pregnancies, so I took a test and, sure enough, ready or not, here comes baby Donahue number four."

Georgie shook her head, so happy for Kolt and Jane. Her brother always wanted a big family, and he was surely doing his part to make it happen. Suddenly, a wave of nausea washed over Georgie, and she could feel the lunch she had eaten earlier start to rise in her throat.

"Falyn, can you take Abby?" she asked, handing over the toddler and rushing out of the kitchen. Sprinting down the hall, she reached the main floor bathroom, quickly closed the door, and fell to her knees, emptying her entire lunch into the toilet bowl. She heaved several more times before she was done and groaned as she flushed the evidence away. Rising unsteadily to her feet, she reached for the hand towel and dabbed at her mouth.

Turning on the faucet, she splashed some water on her face, rinsed her mouth and took a few deep cleansing breaths before staring at her pale reflection in the mirror. *Seriously, this flu is ridiculous. It's been on and off for two weeks, and I just can't seem to shake it.* The towel soiled, she opened a few drawers until she found a stack of hand towels, grabbing the one on top to replace the dirtied towel. Georgie's eyes caught on a lone pregnancy test beside the stack of towels, and before she could stop herself, she reached for it. *Tired, nausea, smell and food aversions. The same symptoms Jane was experiencing. Could I be? Surely not.*

Georgie set it back down in the cupboard and glanced up at her reflection again, her head instantly swirling with 'what ifs.' With a deep breath, Georgie opened the drawer again, opened the box before she could stop herself and followed the instructions, slipping on the plastic cap and setting the pregnancy test down on the bathroom counter. She stared at it. *I can't get pregnant. There's no way. This is just a process of elimination. That's all.* Two minutes later, her eyes still transfixed on the test, a loud knock at the door startled her.

"Georgie, are you in there?" Brooks asked, his voice muffled by the door. "Falyn said you weren't feeling well and had to throw up. Are you okay, Beautiful?" he asked as she heard the doorknob turn and he peeked inside, now realizing in her haste that she hadn't locked the door. "What are you doing?" he asked, slipping inside, as his eyes caught on the pregnancy test sitting on the counter.

Brooks' eyes darted to hers and back to the test as he reached for it. With trembling fingers, he picked it up, his eyes widening and his lips curving into a slow smile as he turned around the test to show her.

There on the tiny screen was the word she once hoped and dreamed but never thought she would ever see. *Pregnant.*

* * *

Thank you for reading Prairie Roads!
Want more steamy romance set in the idyllic small town of Primrose?
Read Prairie Charm now!

ALSO BY TANYA RENEE

Primrose Series

Prairie Sky

Prairie Nights

Prairie Fire

Prairie Hearts

Prairie Sound

Prairie Rain

Prairie Prestige

Prairie Roads

Prairie Charm

With The Band

Finding Direction

Love Notes

On The Edge Of Forever

MORE FROM SERENADE PUBLISHING

Songbird

By Sarah Williams

Brigadier Station Series

By Sarah Williams:

The Brothers of Brigadier Station

The Sky over Brigadier Station

The Legacies of Brigadier Station

Christmas at Brigadier Station

Heart of the Hinterland Series

By Sarah Williams:

The Dairy Farmer's Daughter

Their Perfect Blend

Beyond the Barre

The Outback Governess (A Sweet Outback Novella)

ACKNOWLEDGMENTS

First of all, I want to thank my dear friend, Erica, who without your help this book could not have been written. Your vulnerability in sharing your breast cancer journey with me helped shape Georgie's story in this book and I can't thank you enough for sharing the intimate details of your diagnosis and treatment. You are an inspiring example of survival and resilience, and I am grateful to call you a friend. Thank you will never be enough.

To my husband whom I modeled the character of Brooks after, your ability to make me laugh as I sobbed through writing this story helped me get through it. Thank you for always bringing humor to my life. Pretty sure it's why I married you. And of course, because you're cute. Love you Bear.

To my kids Theo and Raina who fill my life with so much humor and joy. Every day I can't believe how lucky I am to be your mom. You two are awesome. Love you.

To my parents for whom this journey into the writing world would not have been possible. The qualities you've instilled in me through your own struggles have helped shape me into the resilient person I am today. There are no words to thank you enough for all that you've done and continue to do. I love you both.

I want to give you a special thank you to my friend

and a long-time mentor of mine, Cathy Barber. When I made my transition from my business which you helped me build and took a seemingly sudden detour into writing your support in that change meant everything to me. You are a force of nature and one of the kindest, most compassionate people I know. I will forever be grateful to call you, my friend. Hugs.

To my hometown of Landmark, a continued source of inspiration for Primrose. Thank you always!

A very special thank you to my readers who have fallen in love with my quirky characters, my fictional small town and the emotionally satisfying stories I create. Get your tissues ready. This story is going to make you sob one second and laugh the next. I apologize in advance for the roller coaster of emotions but promise this will be a ride worth taking. Thank you for reading! Your love and loyalty are the rocket fuel that keeps me writing!

And lastly as always, I want to thank Sarah Williams and the entire team at Serenade Publishing. There is no one else I'd want in my corner!

9 781764 064620